"A combustible debut novel.... *Your Driver Is Waiting* is a rip-roaring story of family—blood and chosen—fighting to survive under capitalism.... Nuanced in its character development and bold in its plotting, *Your Driver Is Waiting* possesses a scintillating alchemy. It's an upper-cut to the chin of a novel and an instantly memorable debut."　　　—Kayla Kumari Upadhyaya, Autostraddle

"A socially probing, fiercely fun debut novel."

—*Los Angeles Times*

"Enthralling."　　　　　　　　　　—*The Washington Post*

"With a full tank, and rage in her revolutionary heart, Damani drives towards a better world." —*The Guardian*

"A queer feminist retelling of the 1970s film *Taxi Driver,* this one had me laughing loud enough to draw looks on the subway, and that takes some doing. It's a crackling social commentary on the social justice movements of our time, the gig economy, performative wokeness, and who gets to speak on behalf of the disadvantaged. It's a fast-paced read that begs to be devoured."

—Lizz Schumer, *Good Housekeeping*

Priya Guns

Your Driver Is Waiting

Priya Guns is an actor and writer previously published in short story anthologies, *gal-dem,* and
Spring magazine, and anonymously in *The Guardian.* She is a creative writing graduate from Kingston University. *Your Driver Is Waiting* is her debut
novel.

YOUR DRIVER IS WAITING

A NOVEL

PRIYA
GUNS

VINTAGE BOOKS

A Division of Penguin Random House LLC
New York

FIRST VINTAGE BOOKS EDITION 2024

Copyright © 2023 by Priya Guns

All rights reserved. Published in the United States by
Vintage Books, a division of Penguin Random House LLC,
New York. Originally published in hardcover in the United
States by Doubleday, a division of Penguin Random
House LLC, New York, in 2023.

Vintage and colophon are registered trademarks
of Penguin Random House LLC.

The Library of Congress has cataloged the
Doubleday edition as follows:
Names: Guns, Priya, author.
Title: Your driver is waiting : a novel / by Priya Guns.
Description: First edition. | New York : Doubleday, 2023.
Identifiers: LCCN 2022016899 (print) |
    LCCN 2022016900 (ebook)
Subjects: LCGFT: Black humor. | Novels.
Classification: LCC PR9199.4.G8645 Y68 2023 (print) |
    LCC PR9199.4.G8645 (ebook) | DDC 813/.6—dc23/
    eng/20220614
LC record available at https://lccn.loc.gov/2022016899
LC ebook record available at https://lccn.loc.gov/2022016900

Vintage Books Trade Paperback ISBN: 978-0-593-46933-0
eBook ISBN: 978-0-385-54931-8

vintagebooks.com

Printed in the United States of America
1st Printing

For all of us

Dear reader,

Please, always drive responsibly.

If those who have do not give,

those who haven't must take.

A. SIVANANDAN

Your

Driver Is

Waiting

1

If you're going to be a driver, you'd better hide at least one weapon in your car. Especially if you're a driver that looks like me. Not because I'm dashing or handsome, but because I am a woman, of course. I think it has something to do with tits even though not all of us have them. I sort of do, but that's beside the point.

I'd been driving for RideShare using Appa's old car, whose make I will not disclose. I had a switchblade in the glove compartment (which I normally kept in my back pocket), a tire iron under my seat, pepper spray by my door, and a pair of scissors under the mat by the pedals, taped down to avoid any sliding. In the trunk there were six bottles of water, a bucket, a bottle of bleach, some rope, a baseball bat, a few rolls of paper towels, a can of antiperspirant and another of spray paint, some condoms, tampons, pads, and diapers. As humans we have an assortment of bodily fluids and by then I'd tasted about eight of them. In the bucket—and I didn't like keeping much in it—there was a roll of duct tape because duct tape will do just about anything you want it to. I also had some dishcloths, a towel, a crowbar, cleaning products, a toothbrush, baking soda, vinegar, and a squeegee buried under some rags in a corner of the trunk, because things got messy. Oh, and there was a pair of black rubber gloves too. These were difficult to find, but I wanted black.

All the drivers I've ever met say it's crucial to drive prepared. Go ahead and ask one. If they tell you there's not even one weapon hidden in their car, they're lying. As a driver, you have to protect yourself. Out there in the city, we're on our own.

2

I had only closed my eyes for a second and in this new place behind my eyelids, my hair was made of peacock feathers and I was riding a silver pony. The world here was simple. Smiley sun, fluffy clouds, grass that was greener than green on all sides. Then my head hit the steering wheel and I woke up to a long annoying honk reminding me that I was logged into the app, on the road, and in traffic. The driver behind me in a green hybrid flailed his arms around like he was late for his yearly dick suck.

"Fucking drive, bitch!"

"All right, all right. Good morning to you too," I murmured to myself, smiling at him in my rear-view. Of course I am allowed to nap—maybe not stuck in traffic, but if it happens it happens. I'm sorry?

My morning routine was straightforward. I wish I could say I started the day with the four highly effective habits of the wealthy. You know, they wake up at five a.m. and go for a walk without a care in the world. They brush their horses in their stable, masturbate at the breakfast bar in the house they own on their private island that they flew to on their personal jet. But I had too much work to do. I had no kids, no pets—just one job and a whole load of responsibilities. I mean, I'd love to wake up earlier and smash out a few sets. Only, I get home at two or three some mornings, struggle to sleep most nights, and am up again by seven. That's not enough hours to properly rest my muscles, my mind, or even my thoughts.

It had only been about ten minutes since I left the house, and my phone was already buzzing. It was Amma. I hit "end" as I always did, wishing that sometimes it had more power than just ignoring a call. Again and again, her name flashed on my screen, and each time I did the same. Then she sent me the first round of the many messages she will send in a day.

7:57 *We need $350 for the electricity bill. What happened to minimum payments?*

7:59 *Rent. PAY RENT OR WE SLEEP NO WHERRRRRE!*

8:00 *Did U pay last months?*

8:03 *Garlic Causes Blood Clots—<u>click here</u>—SEE I TOLD YOU!*

8:03 *Dont drive like a crazy today*

8:04 *bye*

They say mothers are in tune with their children even if the relationship they have with them is beyond what one might describe as "shitty." Amma was sure that she knew me inside and out when she couldn't even remember how to function like she used to. Somehow, she believed life was more draining for her than it was for me.

3

"That'll be twenty-three twenty-five." She must've been twenty-three herself, and there she was judging me as I glanced at the items on the conveyor one last time. Iced coffee in a can, ginger ale, actual ginger, garlic, onions, cold rub, chilies, Epsom salts, two vanilla protein bars, dates, and some chocolate almonds. Twenty-three dollars and twenty-five cents. I'd need to either do two short rides or one in high surge to make the money back.

"I don't need these actually." I pushed the almonds to one side, knowing I'd regret it later.

The fluorescent lights in the shop were stupefying. I had noticed, in my quick perusal, that the organic foods were no longer in a separate section, but now had an aisle to themselves directly opposite the value options. On the left, a can of baked beans for half a dollar. On the right, a can of baked beans for three-fifty. Someday I'll buy one just to know what they taste like. If they melt in my mouth without a hint of aluminum, then they will be worth every penny. But if you've got culinary talent gurgling in your veins like I do, you don't need the organic shit to make something near-genius.

Row upon row behind me was packed full of boxes,

bottles, and Tetra Paks colored in wisps of every hue: 100% Juice, Completely Sustainable, Ethically Made and Sold by Cherubs in Fancy Dress, No Orangutans Were Killed in the Process, Fair Fucking Trade. Nothing about any of the exchanges in this hellhole were fair. The city was trying to fool us all.

The old woman waiting for her turn behind me smiled while I rummaged through my pockets for another few coins. She wore yellow high socks and held a bag of oranges in her hands, with some milk and a packet of raisins. I was beyond any point of embarrassment that would allow me to care what she or the twenty-three-year-old cashier thought of my grown self looking for more money in my lint-filled pockets.

"You can never find those coins when you need them." I winked at the cashier.

"And don't they just love to hide. Did you check your back pocket? In your shoe? In your bra?" The old woman jested at my expense, laughing jovially at my predicament. She had had her fair share of living too seriously, it seemed—she threw jokes into the air as if she was going to die tomorrow. I plopped the change I found in my back pocket on the counter. I had hid a twenty-dollar bill in my hand and pulled it out from my hair. The old woman slapped her knee with the bag of oranges and I worried she'd fall over. She chuckled and I could tell she had been a smoker. I nodded at the cashier, smiled at the old lady, and grabbed my things. My phone vibrated. The shopping bag with all my twenty dollars and twenty cents' worth of goods probably weighed about four pounds.

Outside there were kids playing in the street. Good for them, I thought. Better than losing their minds in front of a screen. But their motor skills weren't fully formed. Their lanky arms and oversized palms clapped haphazardly into the air, missing their ball every now and then. All I could see were my wing mirrors cracking, and if that were to happen it would be another bill on top of the bills I already could not afford—even with Shereef's discount at the garage—stacked on the kitchen counter.

"Watch it, kids. Don't play near parked cars."

"There are cars everywhere, lady. We're all gonna die!"

Kids these days are so well-informed. I got my phone out. "Hello, one sec, Amma. I'll call you back." Key in the ignition, I took a deep breath. The first of many for the day. A traffic light ahead, a left then right turn before waiting at a school crossing. I could do this drive in my sleep, but I wouldn't, of course.

It was 8:16 in the morning. Mrs. Patrice's bingo started at nine and she was usually my first ride of the day, and my favorite (5.0 stars). She had on her thin taupe trenchcoat with a motley-colored scarf tied round her neck. I could smell her musky amber perfume even as she walked down the steps of her building. She was slow, so slow that most mornings I had time to smoke a whole cigarette before she got to the car.

"Good morning, Mrs. P."

"Morning, Damani. I brushed my teeth before I had my orange juice. Absolutely the worst damn thing to do."

I ran over to help her. Her nails were long and filed to an almond-shaped tip. In my hands, hers were soft orchid petals. Mrs. Patrice shouldn't walk and talk simultaneously, and if you speak to her for ten minutes you can see why. Not when you're eighty-seven and Death lurks at every corner; not if you still want life to spark a light in your eyes. Yet Mrs. Patrice didn't seem to understand.

"Oranges and raisins in the morning are a thing, I heard, at least for people who can't afford prunes."

"Everything's a thing these days. You haven't had any breakfast, have you?" she asked. The fact about old people is, even when they look like they're about to fall to the floor in pieces, they know stuff. Mrs. Patrice held my arm and looked deep into my soul with her milky, cat eyes.

"I'll have something as soon as I drop you off," I said.

It was 8:19. Bingo was only ten minutes away, but from months and months of trial and error, we'd worked out precisely how long it took to get her in on time. Mrs. Patrice needed to put her coat away (eight minutes), pick up a coffee at the breakfast table (four minutes) and make it to her lucky seat (sixteen minutes, by the time she'd greeted everyone she passed) beside Humphrey who was developing an alarming number of liver spots on his face, and Violet who apparently believed heaven was in her granddaughter's left eyeball. This left three minutes for me to get her into the car.

Mrs. Patrice looked through her handbag—an aroma

of lavender bursting free—and handed me her weekly pills, categorized by day, with some floss, Tic Tacs, and a pack of peppermint chews. She didn't use the app, so she handed me ten bucks before pulling out a jam-and-cream-stuffed croissant sealed in its packaging.

"Here. It's not illegal to eat and drive these days, is it?"

"I don't even know, Mrs. P." I opened the door and held her bag so she could comfortably make a nest on my backseat. She leaned forward. Her nostrils flared. She didn't even need to sniff.

"What died in your car this time?"

"It smells?"

"Like a skinned skunk."

I had forgotten to buy a car freshener—I'd have to pick one up at Shereef's. I opened Mrs. Patrice's bag and grabbed a handful of mints. She slapped my hand. I popped one in my mouth.

"It'll stop any nausea. It's an actual thing, I heard."

4

Shereef was in love with Stephanie and thank the gods for that. He was a mechanic by day and a driver at night. Stephanie, who I'd known and loved for most of my life, was a tutor by day, and occasionally a go-go dancer at night. Most people in the city got paid to do one thing, but did something else on the side. Low-paid jobs and unfulfilling work are both exhausting. Even though I just drove, I had dreams that I was saving up for. Driving wasn't going to be my forever, somehow.

"Five years today," I greeted Shereef, who was wearing his sharp gray jumpsuit. The top three buttons were undone, as they usually were, revealing his chest hair and a thin gold chain. He beamed, hugging me as I got out of my car, his hands already soiled with grease. "And look what I brought," I said, chewing dates I wished were almonds covered in chocolate. I passed him the tray, the skins of the dates like thin cockroach skin, the sweetness, a nutty caramel. He took one and threw it in his mouth. We stood outside staring at my car, chomping.

"You remembered, D.," said Shereef, while using his tongue to dislodge a sticky bit of date from his back molar. "It really hit me last year, that I stopped drinking because of this shop." Shereef smacked his lips with each bite. "My shop, Doo Wop, Steph, you." I could tell by the slight glint in his eyes that he needed this conversation; he wanted to dwell on it, but I wasn't going to let him be that sentimental so early in the day. Grinning, I picked up one of the oily cloths on the workbench nearby and stuck out my chin with a sensual pout. I sashayed towards him to the beat of KRS-One playing from the speakers in the garage, the background music to our conversation. I raised my right eyebrow, doing my best impression of Shereef:

"'My grandpa left me five grand when he died. Did I use it to get wrecked? Nah! I put it towards this shop. My shop. Shop of all shops.'" I took a bow.

Shereef laughed: "You're such an ass." He shook his head, showing off his dimples. "Date?" he asked, still smiling, holding out the tray to me. I took one. "But seriously, remember when I used to fix cars on our street?"

"You fixed mine when it was my dad's," I said, coming down from the high of my performance.

"Yeah, I did. He kept it well. Smelled like aftershave and deep fry, but still smelled good." My throat tightened and I nearly choked on my date.

"You got any milk?"

"Five years sober," Shereef repeated while he walked over to the fridge tucked in the far corner of the garage. From where I stood it looked as though he was sticking his head inside it for air. He walked back towards me with a vanilla shake. "I learned how to take apart every bit of my grandparents' 1988 Firebird, then put it back together. That's talent, right?" he asked, passing me the bottle.

"Mediocre talent, maybe. Not rocket-science talent."

"You can pay for that shake if that's what you think."

The garage was in an industrial complex just three minutes from the highway, in an area that lacked all character and charm. It had a color palette that was as inspiring as the dried gum on my shoe. A kid in our neighborhood, gifted with the skill of graffiti, had painted a whole mural on the two garage doors of Shereef's shop, making it a reason for people to drive through the area, even if their vehicles were running smooth. There was a lion in the foreground with a chewed-up leather strap in its mouth, and a Cadillac DeVille classic driving off into the sunset towards the horizon. Of course, you could only see the masterpiece during off hours, so Shereef made sure there was a picture of it framed beside the Open sign because clients were always asking to see it. Beside it, there was a framed picture of the artist. Most people assumed it was there because the boy, named Fonzo, had died, but he was alive and in college somewhere.

Shereef licked his sticky fingers, unbothered by the grease that stained his hands. He walked around my car with the tray of dates, looking up and down the body. "Just an oil change today but you can never be too sure what else needs working on," he said. I popped the hood open to look at my engine. Shereef rubbed the dent near my front lights, placed the dates on the roof of the car, and pulled out his notebook from his back pocket. I was sure he added "*FIX DENT*" on the list of things he planned to do to my car, under my name on the page he dedicated just to me.

"I snoozed a few nights ago. Hit our street sign," I confessed.

"That was you?"

"You see how the sign leaned back? Like it was relaxing for me."

Shereef laughed as he walked towards the garage again, cracking his knuckles along the way, which he did too often. I worried that someday they'd be the size of ping-pong balls. In the garage, all of his equipment was pristine and in place. What he needed was labeled and organized in alphabetical order. He brought out a jack stand, a filter, oil, and whatever else he had in the kit he wheeled over. He moved as effortlessly as if he was making a sandwich.

"I was logged on for more than thirty hours last week, drove for maybe twenty, and I made half of what I would've made last year for the same hours." He wiped his hands with the dirty rag he kept in his pocket as oil spilled into a pan under my car.

"I know I owe you for the past few visits," I said.

"Don't worry about that, but pay attention to your rates."

"I can't feel my legs at the end of the day, sometimes."

"Trust me. No one's getting their usual rate while passengers are complaining fares are up."

"I don't see much passenger info these days."

"Exactly. They're taking money from all of us thinking people don't talk. The rate per kilometer keeps fluctuating and a couple drivers said they haven't been paid."

"What?"

"Yeah, man. People are getting deactivated for nothing, too."

"Like we don't have mouths to feed."

"Trust me." Shereef stroked his beard pensively. "Are you working more nights?" he asked.

"Oh, yeah."

"And it's busy downtown. You notice the protests?"

"Hard not to."

"You see how every day they're getting bigger?"

"Like wildfires."

"Yesterday I saw an anti-sport hunting protest, a climate strike, and one for trans rights all together."

"That's pretty cool."

"It's amazing. I've been thinking, we need to be out on the streets too, you know. Demand higher rates. *Do* something."

"Yeah. Do something," I echoed in a yawn of fatigue.

"Drivers are driving more and making less. I'm *five years sober* today. That's a big deal."

"For sure."

"I know I can do more."

I took the pack of cigarettes from my back pocket and lit one, watching Shereef's two other mechanics with their clients, hoping I wouldn't set off an explosion with my lighter.

"If we want some cake," he said, "even if it's only a slice of it, you think anyone is going to give us some? No one out there is going to feed us a crumb."

I inhaled and exhaled, watching the smoke from my mouth make a billowy cloud above me before it dissipated in the air.

"I guess," I said, because I was completely out of my depth and surviving on flotation devices that may as well have been punctured. Ever so slowly, I was sinking with Amma's voice in the background: *Did you pay the rent yet? Can you turn the TV on? My legs hurt from sitting.*

"I've been speaking to a lot of drivers who pass through here. We're going to have a meeting. Imagine if everyone working in transport went on strike. The city would freeze to a standstill. You keep yawning, D., do you get what I'm saying?"

"Of course. I'm just tired."

"You'll be there, though?"

"For sure. Any time, anywhere."

"We can't wait for a disaster. There's still so many people in this city who are comfortable. As long as they're alright, they don't care about the rest of us, you know what I mean?"

The oil draining from my car came out in a hypnotic stream and I wanted to close my eyes and sleep somewhere just as black.

"My ma threw up on me last night. Probably because I stank of my last passenger's vomit," I shared.

"Ah, that's the smell?" Shereef walked over to his work-bench and brought back an air freshner and some bottles.

"I'll spray some of this new thing I'm trying on it. It should do the trick. Keep it. I'm trying to see if I can sell it somewhere. Make some extra money." Leaning into my car from the driver's seat Shereef scanned the inside, then stopped at my dashboard. With a half-smile he looked at me, shaking his head. I had five half-sucked mints sitting in a row like ducks on my dashboard that I was sure calmed the nausea that the stench refueled and *La Nausée,* as Sartre called it, that came to me in waves. They made my car feel clean somehow, even though they were lathered in my slobber. As I threw my cigarette in a barrel by the garage door I turned back to see Shereef with his arms open.

"We're going to have our cake someday," he said. "Ten more minutes and you're good to go."

5

I couldn't pick up passengers for another hour because of RideShare's break policy (Clause 7, no more than twelve consecutive hours of driving) and because I wanted to make sure I got the evening crowd. I made my way from Shereef's garage back downtown. Driving through the city with my window down, I was aware of my moods. What I saw was how I felt, but sometimes, what I saw was just ugly.

"Wait. Wait!" A woman ran for a bus, propelling her stroller as if she was in a pushcart derby. The bus did not stop for her.

"Hey, sexy!" a man hollered at a woman as she walked by. "What? Can't take a compliment?"

"Do we even have a lighter?" asked a boy huddled with a group of his friends as they tried to rip open the plastic around what I assumed was their first pack of cigarettes.

Gray concrete box after gray concrete box. Flashy buildings sprouted between apartment blocks where the plumbing was close to exploding and the cladding outside could catch on fire with a single spark. Shit will rain on us someday.

"You don't have to go to class today, do you?" A man

who must've had grown-up kids held a teenager's arm as she looked up at him with a twinkle in her eyes. I debated between shouting "Pedo!" or "Daddy issues!" but settled on "He's using you!" instead, because I didn't want to hurt her feelings. But by the time I said it they were well past me, and some woman walking by gave me the finger. Driving as many people around as I do has made me a clairvoyant for determining which couples are meant to be together, and which ones should just stop being. Love is blind, but I'm not.

"Linda, you won't believe it. I'm getting promoted," a man on the sidewalk said into his phone, wearing a suit that was certainly not off the rack. "Vernon says it's about time. I told you, trips to the golf course are part of the job. Drinking late is networking, baby."

Stopping at traffic lights was better than eavesdropping by a water cooler, and I felt myself calmed by the chaos until I spotted a diaper driven over as if it were roadkill, stuck on the concrete creating a speed bump. I sighed. There was a grime to the city, a spillage so toxic it smothered people that passed by. The air was far from fresh, but there we were, breathing in every bit of this manufactured life and asking for more. We couldn't get enough. The city thrived on the dreams of the smothered. As always, I thought about Appa.

6

The sun was out. The glass in front of me magnified the heat. When I switched between foot pedals, I felt a twinge run up from my calf. It strung round my hip and up to my arm. The wheel was pulling against me. My wrists hurt, though not as much as they had when I first started driving. My back ached. I wanted a cigarette. I'd massage my body in a hot bath at night, hoping crystals of salt would heal every twinge inside of me. If that's even a thing. Amma called again. I had ordered her a puzzle, but still needed to buy more word searches, something to distract her. I had already downloaded a bunch of pirated movies and queued them up for her, because when she didn't have anything to do, she called too often.

"What is it, Ma? I'm driving."

"You didn't call me back. I need you."

"What's up? You okay?"

"We don't have bananas. There are only four teabags and I'll use three by the time you come home."

"You can use one to make at least three cups, you know that already."

"I'm tired."

"All right, I'll buy tea. You think you can walk to the

shop today? Maybe try to get to the door at least. Get some fresh air at the stoop. Move your body."

"No. Not today. I have to go now. The TV is on. Where are you?"

"I'm here, Ma. I'm driving."

I never tell people where exactly I am and I won't tell you which city I live in either. In our current times, a city is a place, is a space, is the same everywhere minus the design of buildings, the demographics, and the weather. Cities have all been structured the same. Right now, a few people have a lot, some are just fine, most are struggling. As long as I'm alive, does it really matter where I am? Besides, if the wrong people know my location, they'd find me, fine me, put me in prison for something that wasn't my fault. Am I just paranoid? I don't think so, but I'm getting ahead of myself.

Bananas, tea, a paint-by-number of some kittens in a basket, and chocolate almonds. I needed at least twenty-five bucks in cash by the end of the day for my sanity and my mother's. I couldn't dig into the funds we had to merely survive. It wasn't a crime to spend money on things that made us happy, but most times that kind of money just wasn't there.

I closed my eyes.

The app pinged me. It was okay to drive again.

7

When the stars aligned, driving for RideShare was like driving a confessional. I was an anointed Sister sitting on near-ripped upholstery with Nouveau Car–scented air freshener for incense, and no velvet drape to protect me. I didn't always care to hear passengers' problems, but it occasionally made me feel like a better person to do so. Therapists were expensive and most people these days were atheists. Besides, God doesn't always show that they're listening. For the most part, though, driving was simply driving, day after day, night after night. If I had ten passengers in one morning, half of them wouldn't bother to speak to me, three would be with friends so I was definitely a nobody, and the other two would be anyone's guess. Soul-spillers, secret blurters, conspiracy theorists gone wild. Sometimes there were those who went on about how I was exploited, my RideShare was the devil of all companies, but they had to use my services just this one time.

Cab drivers are expected to have the inside scoop of every city, town, or village they drive in. Us RideShare drivers know the roads, obviously, but most of our passengers don't trust us, probably because we aren't registered cab drivers. In the ranks, RideShare drivers were at the bottom, before delivery cyclists, of course.

A few hours of mostly waiting had passed, aside from three pings. I was at about $19.40 for the day and that was enraging. I'd normally cancel low-paying rides, but RideShare's new policy, implemented out of the blue, was that drivers could not cancel more than two back-to-back rides. All of us were just offloading shitty pings to each other in a desperate game of ping-pong.

I stared at myself in my wing mirror while I waited for a Derek (3.4 stars). My teeth were yellowed, but cigarettes and coffee were too delicious for me to care. They made love in my mouth like it was New Year's Eve and they had no resolutions.

I practiced my smiling, conscious to hide the stains, because if I was lucky my smile would make them hit that tip button (10 percent of which still went to RideShare). Some days it took a lot out of me but today I was in the mood to pull back those muscles and show off those off-white pearls. I looked possessed. I looked constipated. I looked incredibly desperate. I wiped my mouth.

Derek looked rich. He had a turtleneck on and it was summer. Was he pretentious or pretending to be? Beside him, standing about five foot four in camel flats, was a woman maybe six years younger than him, I'd guess. The two of them had rosy skin, flushed from sangria and maybe a midday shot each.

"How you doing, friends?" I smiled, practically ripping my cheeks on either side. I turned so they saw me. My face, my eyes, the things that made me human behind the wheel.

"You don't have an accent! You're the only driver in this city who doesn't," said Derek.

"I'm sure we had a driver yesterday who didn't."

"You're too tipsy to remember. You know where you're going?"

"Oh, yeah. Don't worry," I said.

"I'm almost certain the driver we had yesterday didn't have an accent."

"As certain as you were that you wouldn't talk about our personal matters at lunch today?" Derek hiccupped loudly.

"Sorry to interrupt," I said. "But if you're going to be sick, I've got a bucket in the back."

"Sick? It's fucking one in the afternoon." *Hiccup.*

"I can put some Phil Collins on for you. It'll be 'Another Day in Paradise' and whatever's going on in your stomach will subside. I promise. My ma loves Phil Collins, swears by him."

"You just keep your eyes on the road." *Hiccup.*

"I brought up one thing. It's no big deal. So what if they know you talk in your sleep?"

"Talk in my sleep? You said more than just that." *Hiccup.*

"All right, I'm just going to pull over here and grab that bucket. Can't be too sure about anything these days, right?"

"No, it's fine!" *Hiccup.*

"Because I mentioned that one time you said—"

"Don't even"—*hiccup*—"start Marta. Are you sure you know where you're going?"

I parked my car on the side of the road, knowing that if I stayed there for five hours, RideShare wouldn't even call to find out if I was dead.

"Have you ever cleaned the aftermath of projectile vomit in a car? I'm going to get my bucket." I reached for my door handle, checking for cyclists.

"For fuck sakes. We're going to be"—*hiccup*—"late."

"It'll be a second."

"How can you be this upset? It was one slip-up."

"One slip-up at a work lunch for a merger, Marta. What don't you fucking get?"

"So, I won't get that bucket then?"

"Fuck!" Derek shouted, grabbing the passenger seat and shaking it.

"It's going to be fine, Derek," soothed Marta, who honestly should've just kept quiet because even I knew he was one of those guys that was a ticking time bomb, as composed as he tried to present himself, hence the turtleneck. He turned to face Marta and held her shoulders square with his hands.

The tire iron was under my seat. If things got heated I knew I could reach down, grab it, turn towards the back, and smack Derek in the head with it. Then I realized the pepper spray would be easier, but I had used pepper spray once in my car and learned that it's not a good idea in small spaces. I heard one last hiccup, and then Derek screamed in Marta's face, "I can't stand you sometimes!"

I hit the panic button on the app, thinking he was going to hurt her, but he opened the back door.

"I'm giving you zero stars," he said before storming out of my car like a five-year-old. Marta looked at me and rolled her eyes.

"I've called for help. I can give you a ride somewhere, for free, of course," I said to her.

"It's fine. He'll get over it. Fucking child. Here." She handed me a fifty-dollar bill she had pulled out from her purse and my mouth did this natural thing that could only be called a smile. Marta got out of my backseat and walked off in the opposite direction of her hot-tempered lover. I hoped she wouldn't take him back again. She was too far to hear when I said, "Thank you."

8

Every day I saw how people found ways to get high. Hard drugs, soft drugs, shopping, drinking, sex, fads, and online personas, stretching their phones out in front of their faces, immersed in their tiny screens. People did all sorts of things to feel alive. They were big adult babies scavenging for life, for that sensation, you know, the one that makes you feel just right. But if you looked close enough, sat on a park bench alone, leaned against a brick wall in a dirty alleyway, you'd see people who've stopped to catch their breath. Between the beats of a racing heart full of fear and anxiety, they nearly choke to death.

Jolene would say we could have it all, and I believed her. She was a paper bag I could breathe into while she stroked my hair saying, "Everything will get better. Let me make you a sandwich. With the miche loaf, okay?" Her mouth tasted like grape jam, her bread worth the $18.

I was on my way to pick up a Daisy (4.2 stars), midtown. En route, I drove past a school that looked similar to the one I had attended. Students as young as five were sitting outside the gates holding signs they'd made with crayons, paint, and colored pencils.

WARM YOUR HEARTS, NOT THE PLANET.
Wat's the point of school if the planet is on fire?!!
Frack OFF earthfrackers!
OUR TEACHERS TEARS WILL ADD TO THE
WATER RISING.

That last sign was my favorite because the A-star pupil had cut out a yellow sports car, pasted their teacher's face onto it, then marked it over with a frown using a thick black felt-tip pen. The car was sinking in a pool of blue.

Two streets down, while I was waiting at a red traffic signal, three people crossed the road. First was a man with a tight shirt and well-ironed shorts with loafers and no socks in sight. I wondered if his shoes reeked of nacho cheese sauce. A woman with trainers and a blazer-and-skirt ensemble was close behind him, and then another woman with silver high boots and a pleated dress that had a neon cat puking a bubble of sequins on the front. Someone had sewed every single one of those sequins by hand all the way down to the hem of her frock, and my guess was they were still sitting at their sewing machine in a factory with no windows. How much did the products these people lathered and washed off their faces cost and were any animals hurt in the process of production? In their hands were signs that read

Tech Companies Demand the End of Climate Change
Tech Companies Say Now or Never.

The three of them stopped at the signal on the pavement to chat. They shared a laugh and then they all walked to their individual cars, lined up and parked along the curb.

The light turned green. I was about two minutes down the street from Daisy's, eyeing my wing mirror. A teenager pushed a shopping cart with three kids inside of it. It was one of those moments where one considers calling for help, but the eldest, very knowing, shouted with every ten steps, "We're just running from social services!"

The early-afternoon traffic was gradually growing. Pedestrians had ventured out of offices, institutions, and shopping centers to catch the sun. I flipped on the radio before switching it off right away. I flicked on the air-conditioning, then off, wishing I had a sun roof and could drive topless without having anyone stare at my tits.

I was on my way, holding my steering wheel with one hand and digging through the cubbyhole under my armrest, for a snack, with the other. There was a banana that was much too soft, which I put on the passenger seat. A bag of crumbled pretzels, a lollipop, half a doughnut I'd forgotten to eat. I found a stale granola bar whose best-of date was seven months ago. It was cranberry and orange, with pumpkin seeds. Appa's favorite.

I pulled into Daisy's neighborhood. A woman fiddled with her phone, and then surveyed both sides of the street. Sometimes I got pleasure out of watching people look for me even if I was right in front of them, waiting.

I stepped out of the car after thirty seconds or so. "Hey, Daisy." I waved.

"You have to put a sticker on your car so people can see you."

"I have a license plate."

"No one looks at those these days."

About 99.7 percent of my passengers are just people I offer a service to, despite most of them being obnoxious. Some are kind, a few are good tippers, and a whole lot are forgettable. Not Jolene, though. When she entered my car she brought a handful of stars in with her. Daisy, however, entered like my car belonged to her and she paid the insurance. Slamming the door, she fixed her hair. "You know where you're going, right?"

"Oh, yeah."

"Great."

Sometimes you can see how badly some people need human interaction. There is a clear difference between wanting it and needing it, but I'm no expert. Most people, though, are lonely.

"No, don't go up Main Street. There's people rioting around there."

"The strike downtown?"

"No, no. Around here."

I got a text from Shereef: *Best to steer off Main Street. Sit-in for missing migrants at sea.*

I wanted to go home.

9

It was four in the afternoon. I had to take a break if I wanted to drive at night and the app was there to remind me of that. I waited outside the library where Stephanie taught adults English. She was always telling me about how, in her classes, "Hello, how are yous" stretched into well-meaning sentences that were chock-full of information. "I am fine" grew into how life was in a new country, how tiring it was to answer simple questions, how painful it was to miss home, how i-ron-ic it was to be asked to speak native tongues on a night out by strangers with libidinous eyes. Teachers are therapists, she'd say. It was her slogan.

Stephanie walked out looking as pretty as ever. She cared about her appearance and made an effort from head to toe. Her hair was pulled back with wax so not a single strand frayed from her head. She shaped her baby hairs into waves on her forehead that framed her face into art. Every layer of makeup was set and in place, where colors and gloss highlighted her best features: her cheekbones, her philtrum, her bottom lip, the tip of her nose. Fitting snug around her frame she wore a yellow pantsuit, completely overdressed but delightfully so. Not everyone who looked as put together was right in the head, though.

Stephanie looked smart. She said I looked scrappier. But neither of our majors had gotten us "decent" jobs. Between us we shared an anthropology and a math degree. Now I studied humans from my car and she counted down the hours of every day. We had made it our thing to apply for twenty jobs every three months, but there was a waiting list for everything. A waiting list to be seen, to be read, to gain experience. There was a waiting list to wait. Say that out loud and someone very comfortable will call us complainers.

"Looking fly, banana fry," I said when she opened the door.

"Our photocopying limit is at twenty copies for the entire month now and we can only print two handouts a week. They won't even give us tablets during lessons." She kissed my cheek.

"Maybe we can steal some. I can work out when the Office Depot gets their shipment."

Stephanie laughed.

As usual, I drove us to the park where we'd grown up, which was at the end of our street. I knew I had to tend to Amma soon, but I needed this time first. We had a spot on top of the hill just before the trees behind us grew into the forest. Below us was a park, further down a sports field, a baseball diamond, and then our old elementary school. We walked towards the closest bench, sharing a cigarette and a pack of sour-cherry candy a passenger had left behind.

"How are your folks?" I asked.

"Same as always. They're getting old. And Amma? I didn't speak to her last night."

"Still annoying." I took a puff and passed it to Steph. "You think the kids these days know about the naked man in the forest?"

"Absolutely. There's still bits of his clothes on the branches in there."

"What a guy."

"The playground looks nothing like it used to. Imagine if we grew up with that touch-screen dinosaur thing?" asked Steph.

"We'd probably be better versions of ourselves."

"You think?"

"I mean, look at it." We heard a roar coming from the playground, followed by a *"Touch me, little dinos."* "I bet Eddie Morris's ghost loiters every night wanting to light the whole damn park on fire again."

"He did that with a single lighter, eh! Expelled from all the schools in the area after that." Stephanie passed me back the cigarette and took a cherry from the pack. She sat down and crossed her legs, her back ruler straight. I jumped to the top of the bench, leaning forward with my feet on the seat. Her lips smacked as she sucked the red fruit coated in sugar. She licked every granule with the tip of her tongue, then placed the sweet in her mouth. "Mm. I didn't tell you. One of my students is being deported. No explanation given. Immigration officers just showed up at her place."

"Probably to do with what happened."

"That's what I think. Remember when we used to have to write about the future? In 1998, I thought by now we'd have flying cars and hoverboards."

"I thought I'd be fucking a robot," I blurted. Stephanie laughed.

"Seriously, though." She swallowed before biting the inside of her cheeks.

Every now and then, something happened and people couldn't just sit around. I mean, there has always been stuff happening. So many straws have broken so many camels' backs. But these days, something was different.

On the outskirts of the city, past suburban enclaves and ever-burgeoning trailer parks, well beyond the designated campsites and the sketchy bed-and-breakfasts, there were abandoned cattle sheds. A spectacle in themselves, they were used as sets for slasher films and documentary reenactment scenes on sexual crimes. We did not know this at the time, but a few weeks ago the sheds had been refitted and used by the "authorities" to house two hundred people seeking refuge. But something happened. The reports in most media emphasized that it had been desert dry with scorching temperatures. These days that's all it takes to spark a flame.

"I still can't get over the footage. The sheds were burned to ashes. Surely it was policed, so where were the guards?" Stephanie began counting each point with her fingers. "Who were the people detained? What were they doing there? Where are they now? Why is it that every time I go to one of those protests, I feel like we get further away from any accountability? This is what they fucking do to us!"

"Have you ever burned yourself?"

"From my curler, yeah."

"Getting cookies out of the oven." I showed Steph the small scar I had on my hand.

"The only thing that was reported in the mainstream media was that all of the mysterious refugees were safely deported."

"I don't like the word 'refugee.'"

"Me neither." Stephanie bit the tip of her index finger, the plastic candy packaging crinkling in her other hand. "Some of them were from here too, but that doesn't matter to them."

"Those folks lived here for years," I added.

"Fuck the nation state and fuck the state," declared Steph with exasperation. I held the cigarette in my mouth and exhaled, creating a plume of smoke over us. Steph took it from my hand and dabbed the side of her eyes carefully with her thumb, so as not to smudge her liner. She placed the candy on the bench and stood up, pacing, shaking her head. Her heels tapped on the cement paving blocks. I took a step down and lay on the bench with my legs sprawled at one end. Running my finger over the knots in the wood on each side of me, I followed the never-ending grain. After some time Stephanie grabbed the bag of candy again, and from where I lay, I watched her suck another sweet, struggling with the sour notes on her tongue. I stood up and pawed through my pockets for my cigarettes. After Steph finished work, we normally only smoked one, but too much lingered in the air between us. I needed another.

"Is that Mr. Patel?" I asked, squinting towards the trail around the park.

"I think so. My dad spoke to him last week. Said he's getting divorced."

"Finally. He used to bang some lady on the bench over there when Mrs. Patel went away to India."

"Scumbag."

"Right? Look at him walking."

I passed Steph the cigarette and watched as she blew perfect circles from her mouth. "Mm, we're all meeting at Doo Wop tonight."

"I'll be working."

"Try to come by. Everyone will be there, Toni, Shereef, me—you have to come through. I'll check in on Amma before I leave."

I was pleased that Toni was leaving the suburbs, if only for a night. Toni used to live up the street. She jokes and says she married into the suburbs, but she worked hard, very hard, *and* got lucky.

"You see her new vlog?"

"Pilates for drivers? That was obviously for you."

Toni is a certified Pilates trainer and sells resistance bands with her name printed on them. She spreads her message of muscle function over size and people love it. Only some content creators can make more than a dime, and our Toni was one of them, despite how much she hates to admit that.

Steph threw the filter in the bin beside us and twisted her back around, cracking her lower spine before smoothing out her ponytail. "My dad says Shereef will pick him up from work tonight, so you don't have to. You're not working nights much, are you?"

"Bills are piling on top of the pile we already have. I'm working more than I sleep, and Amma has me waiting on her hand and foot. You know you can cook raw pappadums in the microwave?"

"No. I did not. No word on her benefits?"

We both started walking back towards my car, knowing we didn't have much longer if I wanted to make the end-of-day rush. I didn't have to say this to Steph; she already knew.

"A lady on the phone asked if she's looking for a job," I said. "She can't work now. How can she?"

"Fucking hell." Stephanie bit her finger again. "Your gas is low, by the way." I didn't say anything. Gas, like everything else, was getting more expensive by the month. "Here." She started looking through her bag, fishing out her purse. "Damn it. I don't have any cash."

"Let's get some gas. But you drive." I threw her the keys.

"You know I can't."

"And that's what makes it fun." I started the car for her

from the passenger seat, instructing Steph until she was on the road. On this side of our neighborhood, the traffic wasn't as busy; the after-school rush had subsided, the good kids were already inside doing their homework, and though some others still played outside, they were far from this particular street. I closed my eyes. The car swerved to one side then the other.

"The lines are there for a reason, babe," I reminded her, leaning back comfortably on my seat. A driver behind us honked. Stephanie screamed as if the best moments of her life were when cars drove past or beside us on either side. I opened my eyes, looking for a stretch of open road for a few feet. Seeing there were no vehicles in front of us and no people around either, I said, "Hit the gas a little more. I want to feel alive."

10

I'm not sure which is worse, being broke or being broken. Being both was definitely the worst, though. Appa always said the rich man had the most woes, so much so that he had to buy his sorrow away. He'd say, "Look at how they buy their happiness. Look at how they can't even love. Look at how they struggle to be happy. Look at how they have to fly far away to feel good inside."

But Appa wasn't here and Amma hadn't moved an inch since I last left her tucked under her fleece blanket on the couch. Of course, beside her was a full kettle and her tea, some snacks and food. I wouldn't have left her there the whole day with nothing. I had to be there often, actually. In between rides. In between moods. It worked because I had to pee a lot. Water, it's more valuable than gold.

"You do any of Toni's exercises, Ma?"

"No. Yes."

"I left it on the player for you to find."

"What do you want? I did the hand ones." Amma had applesauce on her face. Food on her face had become her new thing: she didn't care enough to clean herself up and she wanted me to see that. The position of her mouth was now unknown to her because she was that sad. She was fully capable before this, but it seemed as if she wanted me to watch her struggle. When I was young, I asked her if she and Appa kissed on the lips. Her response was a flick to my mouth. "Don't talk dirty!" I had seen them kiss, just once, and I was sure it wasn't an experiment. Amma just loved to lie.

"*Are we poor?*"

"*No.*"

"*Can we afford the mortgage?*"

"*Yes.*"

"*Are we going to be okay?*"

"As *long as you stay in school. Please, stay in school.*"

"*Will you and Appa live forever?*"

"*Of course. How can we leave you here alone?*"

Amma loved watching movies. Her favorites were those cheesy "classics": woman helplessly falls in love with imperfect man.

I pulled the fleece off from her to see if she had wet herself. The sheets were dry but she had a tea stain on the collar of her kaftan.

"I'm not a baby."

"Did you use the toilet today?"

She stared blithely at the screen, trying to mouth the dialogue.

"Did you use the toilet?" I asked again.

"I waited for you. Like a good girl."

She may have been sick, but she was still as sarcastic as ever. We all knew where I got my attitude from.

I put my arm midway around her back and under her

knees and carried her to the toilet. She hit me with her soft little fists. "Put me down. Aiyo, drop me." Amma looked up at me with her sweet, sweet eyes: "Please?"

She had gotten better since it all happened. I had seen my mother with her head against the toilet. Her body was sprawled and lay impotent. The sight of her vulnerability reminded me that she too will die one day. With all my might I'd tried to move her. Screaming, I shook her body. But she didn't wake up. I called for help. The paramedic that arrived had a buzz cut and was well built; he stood as though he was made of bricks under skin. Effortlessly he carried Amma and placed her on her mattress.

"Some jobs are a man's job, sweetheart," he said. Fucking prick winked at me too. That was six months ago. Things were different now. Now, I could at least leave her in the bathroom while I made us both something to eat.

Our kitchen was built for mice. Tiny stove, tiny fridge, and an actual old Easy-Bake Oven that Appa used to bake with. Of course we weren't throwing that out. But then we had a toaster, a microwave, and all the stuff we had when we lived upstairs, owners of our own abode and a tiny strip of land. The issue was that there was no space for it now, so no two people could be in the kitchen at a time. Cooking was a nightmare. Colanders falling from cabinets, broken appliances standing in the way, spices labeled and stacked precariously. As irritating as it was, though, it was home, and I did what I could to keep it tidy. And after dropping off a passenger at a yard sale one day,

I had found the perfect placard, which sat on our fridge to remind us: *Keep the Peace, Keep Organized*.

I warmed the curry and rice I'd made the night before. Yogurt would cool the palate so I grabbed it out of the fridge and filled a glass with cold water. While the food was warming I put the groceries I bought earlier in their place. The extra fifty tip was a godsend I had used to buy Limited Edition Camomile and Anise tea, plus Amma's usual in case she complained about how wrong the new flavor was.

On the side table there was a parcel addressed to me—a new hobby for Amma that I had found in between pings. I ripped it open and read through the homemade leaflet. Red, yellow, and blue potato-stamp designs had been used to create a border around the stippled paper. *Susan's Homemade 5,000 Piece Puzzles: If you complete our puzzle in less than a day, we guarantee your money back!* Amma couldn't walk, but she'd leave me in peace while she was putting Mount Kilimanjaro together with a woman named Susan standing at the top. I left it by the couch for her.

"Damani, Damani," she called from the bathroom.

She stood against the sink with her hands wet. Soapsuds bubbled on the ceramic, fresh and clean, spiraling around the rusting drain.

"The landlady brought your parcel," she said.

"I saw, Ma." My arm was around her back. "Come on. Just a few more steps. The more we try inside, the sooner we'll be out there walking in this wonderful world, having cutlets at Vipran's, and doing groceries like we've got money to spend." She took a step, and then another. She saw herself in the mirror and started crying. I held her. "It's okay. We'll try more tomorrow." I carried her back to the living room.

It's known among my people that food tastes the best when your mother feeds you. Amma sat up on the couch watching some overly excited woman pour her insides out for a man not worthy of her love, while lying to him at the same time.

"Okay, final bite," I said, molding the curry and rice with the last streak of yogurt into a splendid ball. "Ready?" Amma opened wide and kissed my fingers. Closing my eyes, I remembered days that weren't like this.

11

I've been big and I've been small. I was a chubby baby. I never really cared or thought much about how I appeared to others. Appa had said, "It's not about how you look but how you feel, and you, mahal, are beyond beautiful." What made me feel good was feeling strong. Knowing that if I wanted to, I could hurt someone who tried to hurt me added to that. There was enough on my mind and enough on my plate to have to deal with someone else's inadequacies and their failure to handle their own emotions. I could punch you in the mouth and probably knock you out, but I wouldn't ever lay a finger on you unless I had to. That sort of strength takes building.

It has occurred to me that maybe I think I'm stronger than I am. What I can't quite get over, though, is that people don't treat me as they would someone who can lift a hundred pounds on a shitty day. They should treat me better. It takes determination to build up strength, the kind that enables you to lift close to your own body weight, and the kind that helps you to get on by. People see other people and they don't know what they've lived through. They just see what they want to see.

I lay on the floor, facing the sweaty carpet, and did

twenty-five push-ups. My dumbbells felt heavy, but I still did my bicep curls, hammer curls, and then some tricep kickbacks for that defining horseshoe. Progressively overloading after each set is what increases muscle size, so I did four sets of each, finishing my last one with the lightest weights to absolute fail. When I lifted, my arms turned to putty and my mind was put at ease. That was perfection.

On my wall I had a scrappy printout of Meena Raghavan, who was seventy-five years old and still a warrior in a sari, holding a sword as if it was an extension of herself. By the time I'm forty I hope to give fire nunchucks a go and be at least half as cool as Ms. Raghavan. I lay back on the wonky bench that I had found outside someone's drive. The tube light above flashed and then fizzled for a second before it beamed bright again. I was reminded it would cost ten dollars to replace.

A lot of women are afraid to work on their chest because they think only cleavage is sexy, but pecs are another level of fantastic. When my barbell is above my breasts, it's my version of foreplay. With a curve in my back, and my wings together, I benched with a wide grip, and then a close grip, three sets each. Because I didn't have a proper stand, I lifted lighter than I probably could. Safety is priority.

I loved it when my blood rushed. After six months of my workout routine I was addicted to feeling like a throbbing clit. Maybe it's because I grew up seeing veiny men on the big screen kung fu–ing their way through doors that I wanted bulging veins that had their own personality. But apparently that comes down to genetics or steroids, and I don't have either. One time, more recently than I'm comfortable admitting, I drew veins around my muscles and admired them in the mirror.

Getting ready for driving nights involved a precise routine. Strengthen the body, strengthen the mind, meditate. Where I kept my weights was my altar. Sweat dripped from my neck to my chest and my clothes were wet. "Grr," I growled at my reflection in the full-length mirror with my shirt off, flexing as much as I could. The mirror made the room appear larger only from within its frame. Sometimes I could hear the conversations Amma and Appa had had when they slept here.

"What time will you come home?"

"Will you make her favorite sweets tonight?"

If a realtor could describe my room they'd call it "cozy" and then stutter for another superlative. Regardless of the size and old furniture, it was mine. My single mattress was against a wall. My weights were on the side and every now and then I noticed how they rolled, so I knew there was a dip in the flooring. My dresser was opposite. The faux-wood laminate had peeled back on the edges so I had taped it down with bits of duct tape, which stood out below the cracked lamp on top, given to me by Shereef. For my vanity and meditation, my glorious full-length mirror was positioned in the corner, meaning that

I could always see myself, no matter where I was in the room. I went from half-naked to fully stripped down so I could examine my quads and hammies.

Rather than one dedicated day for glutes, I preferred firing them up when I hit the full posterior chain using Toni's resistance bands. With a sip of water I would bloat into a puffer fish, but my abs were getting tighter. Sometimes I wished I could see that same paramedic again. In my own imaginings, he'd be at our door begging for a scoop of protein to which I'd respond with a "Fuck, no." Then I'd shoulder-press Amma above my head, watching his dick bulge at the sight of me. Gobsmacked, I'd slap the man and drag him to the curb outside. Of course, I can't stand most men, if you haven't gathered already. Thinking of it, though, I wasn't quite sure I could actually lift Amma over my head.

Like I've said, I've been small, I've been big, I was a chubby baby. The person looking back at me in the mirror wasn't always the same. Sometimes I put on one face for the day, and another for the night. "Get out of my car." I pushed my shoulders back squared, sucking in my stomach. I stood tall because sometimes my posture was lazy. "Get the fuck out of my car." My upper lip lifted. I was the same character Sylvester Stallone overplayed because didn't he always just play himself? "Get out of my car before I cut your tongue up with my teeth!" The mirror winked back at me. "Get out of my car and give me all your money!" The mirror said no. But we all know, mirrors can be deceiving.

12

There is something about driving at night, stone-cold sober while the world relaxes, that makes me horny. I want it all. The lights, the fear, the surging electricity. The moon watches while the city fills with madness. I am always safest in my car before a passenger climbs in. After that, I welcome madness in, and it pays me to stay.

Light after light, the road ahead was on fire. I prayed I would not die. I could not die. I couldn't leave Amma alone. It was only eight p.m. so there was actually not that much to worry about. For now.

The app pinged me. Pick-up time.

Three little humans stood with their mother, Sonya (3.3 stars) outside a pizza place. Even I knew that Sonya would have a tough time putting those little things to bed with the soda they were sipping on. I drove closer, made eye contact with her and made sure they could all see me smiling. She didn't have a car seat, but my eyes hurt and I wasn't in the mood for an argument.

"Hey, how was pizza?" I asked when the little gremlins barged in.

"We had nuggets, stupid."

"Kenny, don't talk to the lady that way," Sonya said.

"When we go home, I need to study for my science test," said the little human I knew I liked the most.

"Shut up, poo brains," Kenny barked back. It was clear he had an inferiority complex and a lexicon limited to angry insults, all from living under the shadow of his science-hungry sibling who knew how to mind her own business. Presumably. He reached over, stretching his seat belt, and slapped the future scientist on the head.

"Don't hit your sister, Kenny." Sonya held the youngest one close as they were falling asleep on her lap. Kenny's hands were the size of fried chicken drumsticks, and the cup he held was a regular size. A 9-ounce meant for grown adult hands.

"Can you folks be careful? I don't want soda in my car."

"Why does everyone tell me what to do!" Kenny screamed, because he was feeling many different emotions and he didn't know yet how to handle them. Kenny needed to calm the fuck down. While he kicked the back of my seat repeatedly, I prayed. *Dear gravity, do not have your way in my car, may thy will not be done and may all sugary drinks keep off my upholstery, forever. Amen.* Kenny screamed louder and I knew the devil was in him. The scientist joined in because the scientist was also a child, and the new winner of the title for coolest human slept through it all. Poor Sonya was trying to get the other two to shut up, while I was a cooing pigeon trusting that the calm sounds of nature could soothe these children to peace. Maybe I could find a job doing animal voiceovers.

I drove as fast as I could while keeping them safe, of course. Ten minutes later, we arrived at their destination. A $10.40 ride which would've cost more than $20 a few months ago.

"Lady, you suck!" Kenny opened the door thinking his hands were the size of Shaquille O'Neal's. The moment of dysmorphia resulted in that 9-ounce cup spilling what smelled like cherry soda all over my backseat. I clenched my teeth to avoid what was close to firing off my tongue. *Little shit, fucking little worm boy, who will you grow up to be!*

"Oh my God, I'm so sorry." Sonya, who I was about to make 3 stars, was wiping my seat with her baby's coat. "He's had a bad day. I normally don't take them out this late, and . . ."

I breathed.

"Hey, Sonya. Come on. You're a rock star. It's cool. You're doing great. Don't worry about it." I got out of the car and took the baby's coat, wringing it in my hands, hoping this little human would grow to be thirty-five on their next birthday. "You have a good night, babe."

Sonya smiled, and I felt her relief in those few seconds. She fumbled with her kids' bags in her hand with her youngest still in her arms, crying because I guess they saw the state of their coat. I handed it back to her. "You keep safe out there," she said, waving goodbye.

As the happy family walked away, I opened the trunk, got out my bucket, a bottle of Shereef's spray, some baking soda and washcloths. It wasn't long after that I felt my phone vibrate and saw that Sonya had been quick to give me 5 stars. I didn't have the heart to send her a cleaning fee. Looking up, I saw a woman wave to me from the apartment block before a child pulled her arm to take her away. The evening had only just begun.

13

It hadn't rained but the night shone with a glisten; the city was now made of glass. It seemed that the deeper I drove into it, the darker it was, even though there were more lights streaking past me like electric threads. Crowds of people gathered on the road, and on either side, pedestrians skipped along on the pavement. They were on a first date, a first night out, the last one before their supposed freedom was tied down to a contract; matrimonial, parental, wage-bound. I saw a flag that was too familiar. Tamil folks and others in solidarity congregated by the Sri Lankan embassy. Given the number of times I had been wanting to hide my face these days driving through demonstrations, I should've kept a mask in my car. The ones made of latex that were hyperrealistic and you were only allowed to wear in public on Halloween (unless you were an over-enthused white man on a pre-wedding booze-up, of course). In reality, a sheep mask would've been most fitting for me, for sheepishly allowing the app to control every aspect of my life.

Rent was due forty-five days before yesterday, the electric was about to get cut off again, and I needed as many pings as I could get: 5 stars, please, tips in cash if possible.

As I maneuvered on four wheels through the city without being the change I wanted to see in the world, past protest after protest—

Jesus had two Dads!
THE POLICE ENFORCE WHITE SUPREMACY.
I'd rather be in bed.
Arson or climate disaster?!!
O-KKK BOOMER

—then alongside Reclaim the Night for the thousandth time, past a march for taxing the rich where there were also signs for decriminalizing sex work, I felt myself becoming smaller, so much so that I wondered how my feet still reached the pedals. Stopped at a red light, I couldn't count the people passing by, even if I tried. At least in my memory, I had never seen the city like this, especially not at this time of night and it wasn't even that late yet. There was no escaping it—people were out to be seen and heard, however pointless it seemed sometimes. For every moment I was hopeful, there were hours of helplessness that stormed through like a heavy rain.

14

There really is a thud when you hit a body. A thud you can feel from the bumper to the wheel to your seat. Then your stomach drops.

I got out of my car. She was still standing, holding her thigh. Her jeans were a skinny fit, washed-out black but she bought them that way. Her T-shirt was loose and cropped, floating over her midsection. On the side of her abdomen, she had a teeny-tiny heart tattoo. She smiled when she saw me or maybe that was just her face in pain. I could count her teeth. Her sparkling white teeth. I could smell her and I didn't know what that smell was yet, besides the waft of laundry. I don't know all the shades of blond, but I'd guess her's was strawberry, though each strand of her hair may have been made of gold. Her blue eyes glistened, leading me to believe she had never cried a tear in her life.

"Do you speak English?" she asked. I must have been just staring. I still couldn't say a word. I realized I could lose the little I had.

"You hit me," I said.

"You hit me."

"I'm sorry."

"It's fine. I wasn't paying attention."

"Do you want some water? Some pads? I've got things in the trunk—take whatever you want."

She laughed because I guess she thought I was funny. "No, it's fine. Honest." She put her hand on my shoulder. I wondered if she noticed how developed they were. I wondered if she saw my trapezius peeking out from the collar of my jacket. Maybe her fingers felt my biceps. I flexed a little, knowing my bomber jacket gave nothing away.

She started to walk off, rubbing her leg, but then she stopped, turned, and smiled at me. I'm still unsure of why.

15

Shereef sent me a message: *You coming?* Shit. I forgot. He was with a bunch of other drivers and delivery riders working out what we could do about our rates. I could just about make it even though I wondered how much of an impact my presence would serve. It wasn't the pay system, it was the system—what was there to discuss?

I pulled the gear stick into reverse, but from my rearview there were too many people. From my wing mirrors, people appeared closer than they were—the party was over, they were drained or hopeful, but regardless, ready for bed. They had been, at some point, incredibly angry. I sat in my car waiting for bodies to disappear, with my phone in my hands. *I completely forgot,* I started before deleting the text to say, *Stuck in traffic.* I decided not to press "send."

As time passed, a new sort of group crept out, drinking in huddles around already empty cans of beer as they conducted seances for friends who had passed from bad choices. A homeless woman sat up in her sleeping bag beside other people made homeless, sleeping or pretending to. As I waited at the red traffic lights beside night buses and cars, I locked eyes with her—she must have been in her early twenties and had a streak of faded blue hair. I was about to roll down my window, but the lights turned green and I had to get to a spot where there was action. Green lights meant go even if you didn't want to.

The roads were clearing for a crowd who didn't care about traffic rules. The night was lawless. I did a few more pick-ups and drop-offs until my stomach reminded me that I had to eat. Outside Baba's Shawarma Place, which was open late, a small group of people sat around asking for change. I knew they wanted to buy hard drugs because their teeth were black, and their arms were loose tree limbs about to snap off.

"You want extra garlic like last time?" asked the man behind the counter.

"Yeah, and make that two shawarmas, brother. Two for nine, right?" I waited, looking out the window. The people outside were zombies and it was the end of the world. It was funny, but it wasn't. "There's no one to help anyone in this city, is there?"

"It's each one for themselves," said the man, handing me my bag. "And that's exactly how they want it."

16

The young woman with the faded blue streak in her hair was still sitting in her sleeping bag with a book in her hands. I think it was something by Steinbeck. After finding a place to park, I walked over to her, passing a car where a couple was arguing, smelling the sewage in the river.

"You hungry?"

"What do you have?"

"The city's best shawarma."

"Rahim's?"

"Baba's."

"I'm a vegetarian."

"Oh."

"What? Homeless people can't be vegetarians? Leave it on another sleeping bag if you don't want it to go to waste."

"Those guys bother you?" I asked.

"Which guys?"

"Never mind. Just checking in."

"Okay."

"Have a good night then," I said, turning towards my

car. I left the other shawarma on a sleeping bag that was more torn than worn.

"Hey!" called the woman who didn't appreciate my unsolicited generosity. "You can eat here if you're lonely. You got a cigarette?"

I turned back and sat beside her, already feeling warm, wondering if the woman I hit was home safe. I handed the woman with the blue streak a cigarette and ate while she smoked. We didn't say anything to each other. We didn't have to.

17

It was one a.m. Passenger after passenger gets boring, and I've only told you about a few and nothing about what it's like waiting for them all to come through, one ping at a time. I wanted to feel the spring in my mattress, the one that wakes me up mid-sleep. I wanted to feel the cheap bedspread that I loved more than anything else on this earth.

I dropped off the last passenger I could handle for the night, a Rob (4.4 stars) who did a line of coke off his left sleeve and started the ride with "Aren't you too pretty to be driving out so late? Wouldn't your boyfriend get jealous there's a good-looking man in your car? Are you even allowed to date? You're fucking brave! YOU'RE FUCKING BRAVE!"

Then Toni sent me a message: *Out with the S club. Doo Wop girl! Are you coming? x*

I logged out of the app immediately. I had made $103.80 that day, not including Mrs. P.'s $10 fare and the $50 tip I got from Marta in cash. It worked out to near $9 an hour, with my total tips covering expenses. Sure, a day's pay in the hundreds sounds good, but we were chewed up and spat out to have it. I rolled down all of my windows, clearing my car of every single person that had stepped into it that day and night. Nine dollars an hour. I could not do this for much longer.

18

What had once been a distribution center that became too small and fell out of demand, had been repurposed, or so the story goes, by a bunch of us who had grown up in the city.

From the outside, the building still looked abandoned. You couldn't tell it was squatted unless you walked by at night and heard the music blasting from inside. Feral blackberry bushes that had a mind of their own created a fence around the place. Our own gated community, we joked. Through the foliage, you'd find people gathered around the three picnic benches or sitting on the grass, usually enjoying each other's company, even if discussions were heated. You'd notice bikes, unlocked and available as long as you signed them out. Tents lined one wall for those who needed a place to sleep, and there were mats downstairs for when the weather was grim. On another wall were colored bins full of clothes. That's where I had found my treasured army surplus jacket that someone else had culture-jammed by sewing patches over flags and brands, my jeans with rips that were made by falls rather than fashion, a few white T-shirts that were still white, and once even a heavy-support sports bra that fit snug on my chest and mine alone. Enter the rusted metal door and what you hear, smell, and see varies depending on the time of day. The twenty-four seven statement piece was a neon sign designed by a local artist that read: *We are all the vanguard.* In the mornings, with the backdrop of someone reading C. L. R. James or Angela Davis or someone else I don't know much about but should, there was fresh coffee brewing, pastries baking, and people working on projects promising to "make things much better." That sort of genius was beyond me, but seemed to be in motion on the mornings that I stopped by to pick up a coffee. At night, the lighting dimmed, candles were lit, and with the working day wrapping up for some people, proverbial bells were rung to bring in crowds who wanted to let loose, unwind, pray, dance, or do all of that at the same time. This was the only taste of a functioning utopia we had, and so it was our temple. At Doo Wop things didn't operate as they did on the outside. People were different. You could share. You could be ridiculous. You could be you and feel so free just being. Who said communism couldn't be fun?

I pulled blackberries off a branch carefully, so as not to get pricked. I threw them in my mouth before walking ahead, almost hearing Amma's voice in my head: "*Aiyo! Wash before you eat, pillai!*" Familiar faces smoked outside. There was Hugo who had the best Cubans, puffing away on his pipe. Fairy lights reflected dandelion clocks on his tweed coat. He hit my arm as I walked by and I knew he had probably hurt his hand on my biceps. "Check out what I got tonight, tough girl." He flashed me the cigars that sat comfortably in his inside pockets, the lining of his coat turquoise with printed striped seashells.

"I'm good, fam, I'm good," I said momentarily, before turning back. "I'll take two, actually."

Miriam Makeba was playing on blast, her voice soothing my every nerve as she sang "Pata Pata" with that joy she seemed to always have. Even though I didn't understand a word, I knew the dance, because with good music the body knows how to move. I lit my cigar at the entrance before embarking through the hazy mist of body heat, lights, and incense. Couples danced to each other's heartbeat, people let themselves go, and laughter filled the space as the smooth sounds that moved us blared through the speakers. My body swayed this way and that, and I caught a whiff of the toilets every so often so I knew there was another block in the pipes. Luckily there was no water on the dance floor this time. As I held myself, dancing while pinching my nose, all of the passengers I had driven that day ceased to exist. The realization that I wasn't in traffic loosened the tension that wound at my temples. I replayed locking eyes with the woman who held her leg in pain. My inner voice, the one that says things to keep me out of trouble, said, *Do not feel guilty for spending a big twenty on rolled tobacco.*

"You made it." Toni greeted me with a kiss. I danced my way towards Stephanie and Shereef in time to the djembe, smacking wet smooches on their cheeks. "Should I get you your drink?"

"Nah, babe. It's cool."

"You still haven't unlearned it, have you? When some-one asks you if you want something—"

"I can say yes," I teased. Toni kissed my cheek again and I could smell her vodka-and-sage drink. She smiled, leaning against the bar.

"I called Amma. She asked if she could borrow my medicine ball." Toni took a sip from her glass, surprised to learn it was empty.

"She can't use a medicine ball. Don't listen to her." Steph was sitting on Shereef's lap, caressing his ear. He whispered something, and she nestled her head closer to him.

"You're both not working tonight?"

"I finished dancing early," said Steph.

"Took time out to meet—"

"Drivers and riders. I know, I'm sorry I missed it. I had to keep—"

"D., it's okay. A lot came back here tonight. Leila's going to help us out. She runs the activist workshops on Tues-days. You going to stay around for that?"

"It's already so late," I complained. Steph nodded in agreement.

Toni walked over with my drink and another for her-self. "Can we please not talk work of any kind right now?"

"Deal," said Shereef, nestling his head on Stephanie's shoulder as she picked at some grease under one of his nails.

"You folks check out the bulletin board? New workshops on organizing, some sign-up lists for community outreach and—" started a young woman I hadn't seen, who must have just started working at Doo Wop and was breaking all the unwritten codes.

"Can we just get a fucking break?" I snapped with the cigar still in my mouth, feeling horrible as soon as the words escaped. Her eyes grew wide because normally, no one walked through the rusted metal doors with a sour attitude. At least, any sourness was turned mildly sweet at our church.

"We're good, sweetie. We'll check it out later," said Toni, touching her arm with one hand and rubbing my back with the other.

19

The woman who was capable of throwing me off-center, eating up all of my time, and having me smile for no reason at all, was standing in a room full of people. Through the crowd from ten feet away, her eyes peered into my soul and everything inside of me shifted. It's not often we meet someone who can do that, turn our lives upside down with a single look. But there she was, feeling up my soul with her stare. She said, "You're the greatest driver in the city. I love the shape of your arms. Could you hold me, please?" Slowly, she took steps forward rubbing her thigh the way she had when her body met my bumper. Only this time, she winked. It was just me and her. Me and her in a now dark and empty room. Closer and closer. She opened her mouth and I could feel her warm breath on my face. Cherry gum? Maybe it was berry. How was I dreaming about her when I didn't even know her name?

"Damani! Damani! D.! I'm hungry."

It was nearly ten a.m. and I had missed calls from Mrs. Patrice. I realized I could squeeze in a few short rides and still pick her up from bingo if I left right away. I hated the thought of Mrs. P. in a stranger's car and I was annoyed with myself for missing her drop-off trip.

After washing my face I switched the kettle on. Amma was sitting up on her mattress with the television blaring. "You came home late," she said.

"It wasn't that late."

"It was very late."

"Why weren't you sleeping?"

"How can I sleep when my daughter is out at night? Of course I'm going to wait for you."

I went back to the kitchen to make a pot of oatmeal. From my being to all that was in motion around me, the world moved slowly. The water to boil, the oats to soften, my headache to ease. The television was loud in the background.

"The city is in rage and local residents are not happy. Many have complained of feeling fearful of protesters and those gathering in large numbers, worried that violence and looting will spark further riots. The mayor is scheduled to have a press conference this afternoon to address—"

"We need a revolution! Where are the two hundred detainees?"

"As you can see behind me, the situation is intensifying. Rioters are not holding back."

"Here." I put a bowl of oatmeal and honey on the side table and carried Amma to the couch before grabbing the remote to mute the TV.

"It's dangerous outside. You have to be careful. Did you hear what she said?"

I adjusted my jacket in the mirror, making sure I looked good. The outfit for that day: jeans with a rip at the knee from Doo Wop, a white tank top that really showed off my delts, and my bomber jacket, which I found at a thrift shop for $10.50. My black high-tops were waiting for me by the door, because no shoes were allowed in the house under any circumstances. Obviously.

"You have anything planned today? You going to try and take some steps? It should be nice out," I said.

"I want to stay here and watch movies. Can you put on *Philly Live in Paris* before you leave?" Amma slopped her spoon around in the bowl of oats that looked incredibly unappetizing. They needed fruit, coconut flakes, and a topping of granola.

" 'Loose and Smooth' or 'The Final Goodbye' tour?"

" 'The Final.' "

"Any other plans, Ma?" I asked, putting on her request.

"What's the point of doing anything?" she asked quietly, and I had no answer for her. I had no time anyway.

20

I drove fast. No one was around—I'd missed rush hour for once. I slowed down when there were other cars, unless the drivers were young men who drove as if the only real meaning they had in their lives was when they pretended to be drag racers, driving aimlessly up and down the same street to prove they've got testicles. Vroom fucking vroom, they were that vacuous inside. I could understand the desire for speed but not the need for a good-for-nothing obnoxiously loud muffler. You know those guys with those cars, right?

I was heading downtown. Usually, around this time, the city was still taking its time. If there was an hour that was the safest, it was now. At a red light, a man for Channel 6 news stood in front of a camera on the pavement while two others stood holding their phones out, talking to their screens. Another three, seemingly more organized, had someone recording them on hand-held cameras.

"The crowd here at City Hall say they want the government to put a stop to the arms trade. But not everyone in the city agrees," said the reporter for Channel 6. Beside him was a man I suspected was named Tom, and no, he didn't have a handlebar moustache. An elderly woman smoking a cigarette was picking her nose behind them as they were in deep discussion, clueless to the fact that she'd be on television eating her boogers for brunch. On green, keeping precisely within the lane markings, I saw an art installation of white signs that dripped with red paint leading to a statue of some dead white man covered in strips of red paper.

"What do we want? Justice. When do we want it? Yesterday!"

Then came the cavalry, another crowd marching towards the park. Enraged, they chanted, "No more refugees! We want our country back!"

"Keep moving," shouted a driver behind me, even though there were people ahead. When I was eventually able to drive, I noticed how police officers had made a chain around the park. I needed a coffee but didn't have enough time; at this rate, Mrs. Patrice would finish bingo before I got out of the jam.

The traffic light was red, so I waited again. The people that crossed all had a sign in one hand and a big cup of the expensive stuff in the other. I could almost smell their stale coffee breath teasing me through my window. The zest of their freshly dry-cleaned cardigans and chinos, the clean crispness of their lives blowing before me. Those who demonstrated in the mornings weren't the same as those who demonstrated at night. I looked towards the crowd for the woman with the white teeth, hoping I'd find her. I'd ask how her leg was for a sniff of whatever made her smell so clean. I thought, Maybe I should've asked her for her number. Just to be sure she was okay, of course. Though, I did want to stare into her marbled blue eyes one more time.

"Drive, you fucking moron!"

The light flashed green and an impatient imbecile was behind me. Very carefully, after checking my mirrors and seeing that the road was clear, I hit the gas.

21

"You look horrible," said Mrs. Patrice, walking out from bingo.

"I do?"

"I had no choice but to use that app this morning, to find another driver. A Shereef or something." I held the car door open, helping her in. There were a lot of drivers in the city. I was surprised hers was Shereef, but he drove the same circuits I did.

"Shereef was working this morning?"

"He smelled like sports cologne."

"And you smell like a funeral home, Mrs. Patrice. Especially after bingo."

She swatted at my arm.

"How's Humphrey's face these days?"

"He's just one big spot now. He's lovely."

"He'll survive. Let's get you home so you can hop, very carefully, into the shower and smell as pretty as your face is."

"That mouth of yours," she snapped back. "When will you have dinner with me?"

"One day, Mrs. P. One day. You all cozy there?" I handed her the seat belt.

"Let me pay for your next car wash." She patted her wrinkled hand on my backseat as though it was a dead animal.

"Mrs. P., with all due respect, do you need a vibrator? I have an extra one someone left in my car."

She laughed loud and that was perfect. "Look at your cheeky grin," she said.

I wasn't going to take her money. Not unless I drove her for it. I rolled down the window so any smells that may have been circulating would be more faint.

"You're in a good mood this morning," she said.

"You think? I'm always smiling, Mrs. P."

"Not with this smile. Today, you seem a little more mischievous." I laughed, feeling my cheeks flush.

Then she said so brazenly, "There it is. You've fallen in love." Like I said when I started, old people, they know stuff. "Just make sure I'm not waiting around for you tomorrow."

22

Our landlord messaged me: *Your mother is screaming. It's too loud.*

23

....

I've had a recurring nightmare that's haunted me for as long as I can remember. Stephanie's nightmare is losing all her teeth. Shereef's is being buried alive. In mine, I'm on a ladder that stretches out into space. At the bottom, where I've climbed from, there is a pit of fire. The blaze burns each step as I hang on tight to the scorching-hot wood. I move as quick as I can, looking up into a new world, and then a hand reaches down and pushes me back into the flames. I fall and my heart drops, until I wake up paralyzed, unable to breathe.

24

I can't remember driving. I only remember struggling to get the key in the lock and running downstairs.

"Amma! Amma!"

In the past, I've asked the gods if I was adopted because I am not like my mother. The woman that birthed me was sitting, as I had left her, on the couch with the covers over her head. There was a bag of cashews scattered across the floor. I pulled the sheets off her, my body flooded with adrenaline. She had tears in her eyes. "The television stopped working." I took a deep breath in and let a deep breath out. Amma sniffled and rubbed her eyes with a tissue.

I hadn't taken the garbage out yet. Our place reeked of the rotting vegetables lurking in the cupboard. Upstairs, our landlords were having a midday fuck, and I could hear the landlady trying to fake an orgasm with each bang of their bed frame against the thin walls. The lace curtains were closed over the tiny windows that illuminated our space, and the sun outside did little for lighting. This was my life.

I looked to the side of the television and saw that it was unplugged. I walked over to the wall. I had wondered in the past what Amma and Appa did when they had time to fill. As they'd gotten older and worked a little less, I think they were surprised by the time they suddenly had. How do you know how to live when you've never been given the freedom to? Amma watched me hold the cord up. The remote was on the floor beside it with the batteries scattered nearby. I looked at Amma and she held my stare. I had never had to give her motherly eyes until recently. I usually just kept my mouth shut.

"You watched a Michael Douglas film?"

"I don't want him to die."

"He doesn't have cancer anymore, Ma."

"All thanks to my prayers."

"You know he doesn't even know you exist, right?"

"It doesn't matter."

I rolled my eyes, knowing there was more on the way.

"You don't even know what today is!"

"It's . . ." I began. And maybe if Appa were in the room with us, he'd have had plastic roses in his hands as he always had on their anniversary, because plastic lasts forever, he'd said, and it helped that each stem was sold for a hundred pennies at the value shop. He wouldn't be so mad at me for forgetting. "Your anniversary. I know, Ma," I said.

"Where are you going? What about the TV?"

"I'll make lunch. We'll eat together. Then you can watch whatever you want."

"No deviled beef, okay?"

I heated up some food and began to feel myself coming down from the fear. Each day was a copy of the last one: watching the food as it heated, or cooking it. Feeding Amma, or running home in a scare. Picking up more shitty passengers and being too tired to even see Shereef, Steph, and Toni. My phone buzzed. It was from RideShare: *You sent us a panic message! We're sorry. What is the panic? Did you have an emergency? Do you need urgent assistance? We're always here to help.*

Fucking Derek.

25

There is a sadness I feel and don't often talk about. I don't know how to fix it. It doesn't excuse anything, but to add to all that, times were rough. The sun rose, the sun set. Cars rolled past me, and people carried on. I don't know why we're born, but I think a lot of people waste so much time not thinking about what they could do to make the world a little better. Make their own lives a little better. Even though I didn't know how to make mine any better than it was. I worried that I would die in my car. That I would die unfulfilled. Or that I would die and not know what an easy day felt like. I worried that if I ever did, I would still not be happy inside.

I tried to forget about the traffic that day, and every person I saw some hours past. They were shadows pulling each second behind them. The woman I had hit, though, annoyingly still sparkled in my memory. I had replayed the sequence of events with her, over and over again imagining scenarios of us talking in different circumstances. It was late, and I was on the road, but something about her soothed me.

26

It was 2:15 a.m. and the club I was parked nearby closed at 2:30. I hid out opposite an alleyway where I saw teenagers throwing bottles at a window. Glass shattered on the ground and I wondered what it would feel like to put shards in my mouth.

Before the D.J. killed the last track I thought I'd use the minutes I had. Fussing with my seat belt, button and zip, I put my hands in my pants. In my underwear, it was warm and moist, and I was suddenly taken to a feeling called home. I smelled the tips of my fingers, inhaling the bliss from lemon detergent and pussy. I was safe and welcome in my tank-near-empty-again car. The whiff was better than a line of coke. I'd masturbate after work, thinking about oiled breasts and pecs, sliding slippety slide off my body. I'd do twenty-six push-ups, crawl back on my mattress, and come again, shooting myself out onto the moon. Before I could even give myself a little taster, I got a ping. Steven (3.6 stars).

"You're my driver?"

His pupils were so dilated they were oil stains. He had a yellow coat on. His friend was wearing a leather jacket. Their weight pushed the car down as they got in and their energy made me take my seat belt off, just in case. I didn't want to get strangled.

"You know where to go, right?" asked the man with the leather jacket. His eyes were an angry gray and I remember because I can still picture them when I close my eyes.

"Yeah, I'll get you both where you want to be, safe and sound."

The man with the yellow coat started catching things in the air. "Sounds. Do you hear the sounds?" Leather Jacket closed his eyes, smacking his lips. "Do you see it?" Yellow Coat asked, directing his question to his friend. But Leather Jacket was somewhere else behind his closed eyes. "There's a pink bird on your dashboard, driver. It's talking to you."

"Can you tell it to keep quiet, cuz I'm driving and it's late."

"You have a nice voice," said Leather Jacket. I didn't take hard drugs, but I knew this much: it was never the drug, but the person. It was never the weapon, but the intent. He leaned forward, his chin resting on the corner of my seat. He stroked the upholstery. Yellow Coat tried catching the bird. Leather Jacket smelled of expensive cologne drowning in sweat and piss. It amazes me just how much of a stench drunk people exude when you're stone-cold sober at two thirty in the morning. He leaned forward some more. I felt his hot breath first. Then his lips on my neck.

"You'd better move off of me," I said. I was already bombing along, and this was exactly why I didn't like driving on the highway with passengers and exactly why I didn't like working nights. I couldn't stop to grab the tire iron and use it with two of them in my car. Yellow Coat's foot was close to my handbrake, and my body was stiff. I had the switchblade in my pocket that night, but there were a lot of trucks out and they all felt too close to make any sudden moves.

The man's tongue was on my skin. He reached his arm around the seat and his hands looked for my breasts, gripping my body along the way.

"Get out of my car. Get the fuck out of my car!"

"You're driving," whispered Leather Jacket in my ear. "Remember, you gotta keep us safe."

"The bird, the bird." Yellow Coat's hands grabbed for things no one but he could see. The next exit was only a minute away, I just had to hold on. Just hold on.

27

The next morning, there was traffic. Coffee beans that were grown far away and sold for pennies were ground and served for $6.50. The silky black gold was poured in tall beakers and sipped by people who had a lot more money than I did. Their fuel made the air smell delicious.

This part of the city used to be cool because it wasn't, but then it was forced to be a different kind of cool. A pricey one. I think they call that *gentrification*. There was something about the house I was parked outside of that made me want to go inside and have a long bath. I could almost feel myself sinking into the bubbles.

The woman who opened the door had blond shoulder-length hair. She was the woman I'd hit. Her rating was a solid 5 stars. Of course it was.

"Hey," I said, as cool as a frozen cucumber.

"Hi." She smiled. She stepped in my car with that handful of stars and a whole entourage of celestials trailing behind her. She had freckles on her nose I hadn't noticed the first time I saw her.

"Do I know you from somewhere?" I asked. She

looked close at my face and I saw how the memory of me startled her.

"Oh my God."

"You were at Shonda's party?" I lied.

"The other night—"

"That was you?"

"You hit me."

"Oh, right. That was *you*. I saw you and drove right into you."

Her cheeks reddened to the color of her lips, and I was hit with the want to kiss her. She laughed. I smiled, watching her.

"I hope that's not the case." Was she flirting? I nearly forgot to start the engine. She was beside me, around me, and then at the back again. Her presence danced throughout my car.

"It's busy in the city today."

"Yeah, a lot of us are out there."

"A group of you?"

"I mean, everyone is protesting."

"The good guys and the baddies."

"I don't think the world is that black and white. But we're the good guys," she said.

"I'm sure everyone out there thinks that about themselves."

"You don't think I'm on the good side?"

"Life isn't a movie and you aren't a superhero, babe."

"No, it isn't, and I'm not. You're right. Babe."

"You ever notice how the bad guys in movies actually have the best ideas for the betterment of society?" I said. "But it's the superheroes who stop them from changing the world."

"What?"

"I'm sure you're someone's hero."

"Want to be mine?" She looked at me as she said it, and I felt a jolt course through my body.

"Well, you don't even know me. Maybe I've got a body in my trunk."

"Who doesn't? Maybe I save the whales all day so that I can be bad all night."

"Sounds like something I'd say. Do you like pancakes?"

"I prefer yogurt and fruit in the morning."

"Do you sleep on your stomach or on your side?"

"I sleep on my back."

"It's better for you."

"It is."

I looked at her in the rear-view. She held my stare. Other people had tried to do so while sitting in my car too, but I usually didn't make space for it. She blushed, not suddenly, but when it was right. I laughed. She made me laugh and I liked that. I looked: her face glowing, my heart beating. She took out her phone. She was probably telling someone about the creepy driver in the car and I nearly took the wrong left.

She's no big deal, I told myself, aware of what I was capable of. I felt lighter on the shoulders. They rolled back. My jaw loosened and I remembered I had a four-pack, sometimes six- depending on the lighting. "Any big plans today?" I asked.

She thought, as though she cared enough to answer.

"Well, later I think I may run a hot bath. Have some wine."

"Is that an invitation?"

She laughed and her eyes sparkled when they caught mine in the rear-view. She touched her face and pushed some of her hair behind her ear. Her hands held the seat in front of her as though she was familiarizing herself with my space. She rested her head on the headrest in front of her and looked up at me. Who does that unless they're falling in love?

She ran a finger down the window.

I stopped the car at her destination which was, frankly, unjustifiably close to her home, but I knew she wasn't lazy. I just knew it. She stayed seated, then looked at me.

"Opening doors is not part of my services, sweetheart."

"Oh, for sure. I was just thinking of something. Wait here for a bit."

Before I could respond to her demand, she was out of my door and pushing her way into a place I'd never noticed before, Mademoiselle Ethiopia Café. I thought I'd have to try hard not to look at her ass, but I just watched her as she was, walking away. I grabbed my phone and ended the ride, my brain still in a trance from whoever it was who had just blown through my backseat.

Darling, could be the love of my life, knocked on the

window. She had two cups of coffee. "This is for you, because you made my morning." She was so pretty with the sun in her face. Her eyes were glass beads. I really wanted to kiss her. On the cheek. It wasn't often I met anyone who made me forget that I was their driver, or realize that I was a person. I didn't know how I made her morning—did she try this hard with everyone she met?

"Go out with me. Would you like to?" I asked.

"I'd love to," she said, too quick. She licked her lips and thought for a second, looking straight at me. "I'll give you my number."

I handed her my phone. "I didn't ask you what your name is," I blurted.

"It would've appeared on your phone."

"I was distracted."

"I'm Jolene."

"Jolene?"

"Jolene. But you can call me Jo."

"I can do that. Jo."

"Hey, some friends of mine are hosting a fundraiser here tomorrow at six. You should come."

"Do you want me to pick you up or—"

She laughed. "I'll be here, Damani. But thank you." She remembered my name from when it first appeared on the app under my mugshot. She held out my phone and when I went to grab it she pulled it back first, like the biggest tease of the century. "You're funny," she said, before turning and heading back into the café without so much as a glance over her shoulder.

28

"So it's a date?" Toni's voice boomed through my speaker while I drove. I had told her about Jolene. Sure, I had a passenger in the car, but this conversation was important. Besides, the kid in the back was wearing earbuds and his eyes didn't leave his phone. I enjoyed giving rides to kids who were older than Kenny and the screaming scientist, but I couldn't stand teenagers. Teenagers were menaces to society. They fiddled with my door handles, spat when they spoke, and were so damn loud. They felt rebellious when they didn't wear their seat belts. I have been tempted to slam the brakes when one of those little shits tried giving me a hard time just to make themselves feel cool in front of the other pubescent gremlins beside them, all dangly, hormonal, and insecure. I've imagined the most irritating of my teenaged mutant passengers flying through the windshield. When they are alone, they are nothing. When they are in a pack, I want them all to die. (Of course, I don't mean it literally, but who hasn't ever thought it?)

"I think so," I said. "I haven't been on a date in a while."

"You'll be fine. Just don't . . . I don't know . . . Don't—"

"Is this going to be encouraging?"

"Just be yourself," said Toni.

"How inspirational."

"I love you, that's all it is. So what's her background?"

"White girl."

"Okay. That's okay."

"For sure. But she's not like Stephanie's cousin, Courtney, white."

"She's rich girl white?"

"Prosecco every Friday white."

"Is she actually?"

"Walks like it."

I heard Toni thinking through my speakers. "Well," she started.

"Listen, if I died right now—"

"I'm knocking on wood."

"She would plan a better funeral for me than any of you can."

"I'm offended, D. Does she even know you want to be cremated?"

"It wouldn't matter."

"My brother is a caterer. Your funeral food would be so bomb you'd be resurrected."

"She'd have party favors for everyone. Personal-sized goodies and silver lockets with the best pic of me slapped inside. She's that kinda white."

"You'd choose party favors over your own resurrection?"

"Well—"

"Please, don't answer that. So, you're messing with her for a five-star funeral? That's classy."

"Oh no, T! I love me my two stars, happy to settle for three. Rate me five, though," I said to the boy sitting at the back. He nodded, still immersed in his phone. "You know that I know funerals are expensive."

Toni sighed. "I know, babe."

"Her and I are different."

"Well, you just met. See how it goes."

"Yeah."

"It does sound like you're hiding the fact you're cunt-struck, but hey, no judgment here."

"What? Come on!"

"Kiss me right now in the backseat vibes?" Toni teased. The boy in the back chuckled.

"There were actually sparks flying in my car."

"Mm-hmm."

"And she is organized. She's out there demonstrating."

Toni laughed. "Just enjoy the date. See what happens." Maybe I was jumping the gun a bit too quick. The coffee Jolene bought me was still in my cup holder. "Will she be the first person since . . . ? I just don't want things to end the way they did with the last one."

"That was because she—"

"Talked shit about your food truck dreams. I know."

"No! Because she tried to steal a hundred bucks from my house."

"Oh, yeah! I forgot about that," admitted Toni.

"See. People don't ever remember the whole story."

"Sorry, babe."

"And yeah . . ." I glanced at the kid in the back again. "There *have* been others since," I whispered.

"Just fucking doesn't count. You're making a face, aren't you?"

"My face is my face. Listen, I have to go. People are driving like maniacs. Love you."

"Be careful! With everything." Toni blew a kiss which hit me right on the cheek through my speakers. The boy looked up from his phone and at the road. He caught my eyes in the rear-view.

"The roads are fine."

"Mind your own business, kid." I pushed the clutch down, then shifted gears. When I go fast, I am invincible. I pushed the gas a little more. The boy didn't say another word.

29

Dr. Thelma Hermin Hesse made weekly videos sitting in front of a virtual background with one of her three cats on her lap. Each video was a surprise. Black cat, white cat, or tabby? Dr. Thelma Hermin Hesse was my therapist. Well, she had thirty-five thousand subscribers, so she was all of theirs too, and anyone else who tuned in to her free content. I opened my laptop and her voice resounded throughout the bathroom, picking up from the last video I had watched. *"Four, three, two, one, breathe out. Excellent. Let's do that again. Breathe in, one, two—"* I clicked on another video; my breath and heartbeat were running in good time. The fundraiser was in a few hours, and what I needed was guidance. Dr. Thelma Hermin Hesse was sitting with her black cat in front of a visual time lapse of sunflowers growing from seeds. The title of the video was *Because You Are Actually Worthy* and the thumbnail was Dr. H. with her hair down, rolling in perfect waves off the screen, with thumbs-up icons plastered around her face. My computer was on my lap as I sat on the toilet. In her most soothing voice Dr. Thelma Hermin Hesse said, *"It doesn't matter what has happened. It doesn't matter how you feel. You're worthy of good things. You're worthy of love, friendship, kindness, and new beginnings. Be open to it. Chin up. Smile. This is only the beginning of the rest of your life."*

30

I had never stepped into a Mademoiselle Ethiopia Café, but I could tell that night that it had been made over to look even more uppity yuppie than usual. The decor was judging me: fresh bouquets in vintage glasses that were the size of club-sized pickle jars scoffed at my shoes, the votive candles that floated in midair knew my bank balance. Platters of food were laid out for royalty; I worried my breath might turn them to poison. Kings, queens, and jesters ate with recycled wooden cutlery in a humble attempt to save the world, while their branded clothes hid their well-fed stomachs. The focal point hanging over our heads was a glass chandelier that twinkled, gently swaying me into a fantasy of, This could be your life minus all the pretentiousness. I nearly gagged at the seven different types of hummus—in papier-mâché bowls made from news clippings. Clippings and stories layered upon others for $45 made by some chick named Caitlin. I wished I'd brought some old food containers, because surely there would be waste. No amount of people could ever eat that much hummus in a single night, however much they loved hummus. There are other great foods in this world. Hummus deserved a break.

"Loosen up, good people, the evening is just getting started," said the D.J., who balanced a monocle on her left eye. She spun Putamayo classics, whale wails to some dude on the bongos, flamenco that wasn't Paco de Lucia, and loads of the Beatles. I swear to you, "Imagine" was played after every other track. The air was full of imaginings with no plan to take action—or was that my problem with the damn song? If John Lennon would fuck off for just a second, I could've regained my thoughts. How could I imagine a better world and then let it all be at the same time? I took a deep breath in, and then out again, waiting for the D.J. to notice me watching her as I nibbled a celery stick dipped in red-pepper hummus. When she saw me, I gave her a thumbs-up and mouthed, "Brilliant tracks!"

The most astonishing addition to the soirée was an enormous cheese board at the other end of the table. I had never realized how many different cheeses there were, and how much could fit on a single board. I was a mouse with an expensive appetite. Everyone knew I was there for a nibble, but it didn't stop me from indulging in the menu. As I made a sandwich entirely out of cheese—a piece of fontina, with a layer of fig jam, a slice of manchego and some tartufo to top—someone tapped my shoulder. "There's singing outside."

I followed the woman to the back door with my cheese creation stuffed in my mouth. It must've been the transition from the moody lighting into the dusky bright, but I didn't notice just how big the beads on the beaded curtain were. A peach stone nearly knocked my left eye out.

A young man with a platter noticed. He smiled. "Cava?"

"Do I have a what?"

"Cava. Sparkling wine. Want some?"

Glass in hand, I headed towards the patio. Around wildflowers in terra-cotta pots people were gathered, half-smiles plastered on their smug faces, eyes closed or merrily open.

"This is touching." The woman who had informed me about the singing held a lighter and waved her arm in front of the choir who was belting out something about joy and summers. I saw someone I thought I could speak to, a Gujarati woman. She was taking a photo of the moment and from her air and dress I guessed she had a nice house with wisteria that grew on the west wall. In the winter, when she opened the windows in her master bedroom she had the spring to look forward to for a new season of lilac blossoms, as logs burned in her fireplace and mulled wine warmed on her stove. Sip, sip, crackle, is what comfort sounds like, with the knowing that good days were constant. Life, a living dream.

"What's this about?" I asked her.

"They're singing for all the dying children."

"In the city?"

"In Africa."

I didn't say anything, but as if she heard my thoughts she said, "At least they're doing something," then walked away, her floral perfume tickling my nose.

I said loudly, "No, I think it's wonderful," but she was a fast walker and seemed to not want to be seen with me.

I had never been around so many white people before, and they weren't akin to the white people I knew from my neighborhood or area. I had plenty of white friends growing up. All six of them that went to the schools I went to. I had never been around Black and Brown people that warmed to these sorts of spaces either. As similar as some faces were to mine, they weren't like me. What the fuck was I doing here?

I had a brandy, and then another, and went out for a few smokes, all the while wondering how I could even begin to explain this experience to Steph and Toni. I'd start with the cheese, I thought. No, it would be the hummus, of course. I'd have to draw out a chart: us with no income, us when we could work, us in our dreams age thirty, Jolene, and the people who were putting envelopes in that red donation box because apparently bank transfers weren't so fancy. I could almost hear Shereef screaming, *"It's the haves and the have-nots, there's no in between! You either get it, or you don't!"* And then I saw her. She wore an olive-green dress that hugged her waist and flared out past her knees. The back was open. *That's* what I was doing here.

I watched Jolene as she hobnobbed effortlessly, rubbing shoulders, smiling with ease. She had an earpiece fixed to her ear. Eventually, she saw me and waved, mouthing, "One sec," every time someone approached her. In one instance, it appeared she mouthed, *"Want sex?*" She winked right after, too. While I waited and lingered awkwardly, watching people waylay her from me, I attracted friendly folks keen to mingle.

"Where are your parents from?"

"Isn't it horrible what happened to those refugees?"

"Have you been to a demonstration?"

"It's all the people out in the countryside who bring the entire country down."

"I'm afraid for my friends."

"My boyfriend is Chinese. My mother, a bigot."

"The conflict in Israel is really upsetting. I partied on Tel Aviv beach once and Gaza was literally right there. I still have nightmares. I'm in therapy, did I mention?"

"My partner and I are opening up a vegan bakery. The space used to be a noodle shop, ran for about thirty years, so the kitchen is all set up, and we just got in the new curtains."

"Are you investing in The Fight?"

"I've been to twenty-five protests in the past two weeks. I am literally exhausted."

Question after question, comment after comment, painful attempts to make small talk great talk. I was poised, likeable (I thought), contained as in I was on a level of myself I knew was manageable to those around me. Of course, I grew up knowing what spaces I could fill, where I needed to be slightly smaller, and where I could truly be myself. Usually the latter was in spaces where there were no people, or at Doo Wop. The chandelier spun and no one noticed. Lights flickered off the glass and onto the walls reflecting streaks of rainbows that flashed in seconds. A part of me sat on the ceiling watching people eat hardly any cheese off the cheese platter.

"It's completely unacceptable that our government is making no effort to change things for all the people out on the streets demonstrating! All of us!" shouted a woman on a microphone by the D.J. booth. "If we want a better world, we have to make changes to our lives." Everyone clapped but I couldn't hear their hands touching. "We're launching our much-anticipated new brand of spring water, with what better name than The Fight." People's mouths moved, suggesting they were cheering, and their hands waved in celebration. "Ten cents from each bottle goes towards a breakfast plan for a kid here in the city. Sixty cents goes to save our oceans! We've been so lucky to be sponsored by Cee Lo Drinks Limited, so let's fucking celebrate tonight and use the power we have to make a . . ."

"Change!" everyone roared, so loud I felt my heart hit my chest for a second. My lungs puffed and all of the air inside of me was trapped. I saw myself watching everyone, looking for a human reaction in their faces. I clapped with the people around me. I smiled when they smiled at me, wondering how it felt to be so free. I really should've just worn a sign around my neck: *Will talk for $30.*

"I'm so glad you made it, Damani." Her voice snapped me back into my body.

"You look good."

She reached in for a hug, but I held my hand out. She laughed and shook my hand with a tight grip, maintaining eye contact the entire two seconds. Her fingers caressed my palm as she let go. Her hair was in a low bun that sat on the nape of her neck. Her cheeks were brushed with a punch blush and on her eyelids she had smeared a gray shadow under a thin black liner.

"What?" She smiled, running a finger over a brow. "I . . ." She laughed, aware of what her stare could do.

I bit my lip in embarrassment, watching her tongue trace her top lip as she smiled with her mouth slightly open. I laughed and regrouped. "So, this is interesting."

"I hope you're okay. Some of the people here are . . ."

"Characters."

"Yes! Excellent." She laughed. "Certainly a lot of characters here. They know how to donate, though, even if they're slow learners. It's a process, right?"

"For sure." I nodded. "What about that guy over there." A man stood ten feet away from us wearing cargo shorts and a Hawaiian shirt with a black beaded necklace around his neck. "How much does a guy like that donate?" Her smile was playful as we watched the man drink his beer slowly, looking for someone to speak to.

"He can definitely afford a better outfit."

"I mean, that's what I was thinking." She laughed.

"He's actually very humble."

"I bet he is."

"And we need as much money as he wants to give." I

laughed this time and saw that Jolene was still examining the man, mischievously with a smile. She leaned close to my ear and whispered, "Tonight, he wrote a check for five thousand three hundred and fifty-five dollars and fifty cents," her lips brushing my ear.

"He couldn't just round up to the next dollar?"

"He has to offset his tax somehow." She laughed to herself. From my peripheral vision, I saw how she studied me.

"What is all this about anyway?" I asked, looking around before making eye contact again.

"We're fundraising," she said.

"What for?" I put my hands in my pockets, feeling the warmth of my thighs. Keep cool, keep suave.

"Well, there's so much going on in the world right now and the city is practically on fire. Most of the funds will go towards an environmental group, some for school meals. We want to actually do something and keep people involved."

"Of course."

A woman with a clipboard butted between us.

"So at eight o'clock, there are a group of police officers that usually come for dinner and coffee. We're going to blast music at them," she said to Jolene.

"To scare them away?" I asked.

"Kat, I was talking to Damani."

"Oh my God, I'm so sorry," said Kat, turning around to see me. "So the music thing?"

"Why would we do that?" answered Jolene.

"The committee already agreed to it. I'm just keeping you in the loop," whispered Kat.

"Fine." Jolene looked at me and rolled her eyes.

"Fabulous! And at ten we're turning off all the lights for the climate crisis."

Jolene's eyes widened, perplexed; her lashes were neatly fanned.

"Okay, we'll do that then." She was clearly vexed, and I liked that.

"Exciting!" Kat scribbled some notes on her clipboard. She looked up at us and forced a smile while her eyebrows raised simultaneously. Then she walked away.

"I noticed people have wristbands. I didn't pay for a ticket," I said, reaching for my wallet. Jolene held my arm to stop me, then ran her hand down my forearm, locking her fingers between mine before pulling them away like satin ribbons tickling my skin.

"You're my VIP," she said.

"I think this is great. You're doing great, Jolene," I said, despite my reservations.

Her smile was soft and flirtatious, the freckles on her nose perfect. I wanted to pierce her nostril with a nail. "Have you had a good time so far?" Jolene's face was superimposed onto a background of blurry faces.

"Yeah. A rocking time," I said, experimenting with new phrases, trying to fit in. Jolene held in her laughter well.

Maybe she had felt my discomfort, because she asked, "Do you want to go for a drive? Just me and you."

Or was this a test? "Maybe later," I replied. "It's nice here, and I know you have to make sure things run smooth." I squeezed her arm, and we locked eyes. I wanted her to know I was okay, even though everyone kept asking me to repeat my name when I introduced myself. I was used to this.

She tinkered with her earpiece, listening to someone not too far from her tell her that they were running out of Swiss cheese. Then three people walked over who smelled like perfume that cost more than sixty a bottle.

"Jo! We've been looking for you. This is fantastic. The people you're helping will be so grateful."

"*We're* helping," she corrected.

"What would they do without us?"

White noise crashed into waves and whale sounds, and I was biting my cheeks.

"Honestly, I've been wondering what I can do with all that's going on. I've been reading loads, Jo. That reading list you sent out is brilliant," said a woman in a pink blouse.

I reached to touch the fabric and wondered if it was the skin of a dove. "This is such a gorgeous blouse," I lied.

"Thank you!" She was surprised.

"It starts with all of us," another woman was saying to Jo. "We have to do something. We can't just watch it all happen like this."

But what were they talking about? What did they actually want to make better? Jolene looked at me as the woman spoke to her, mouthing, "I'm sorry." The walls vibrated as more people walked over to us. I saw myself hold my head. I saw myself move away from them. Then I heard, "This is my friend Damani. She's—" Jolene's mouth moved but I only heard whatever wind instrument the D.J. was playing. A woman looked at me approvingly and I could tell she fancied what she saw because from looking as I did for thirty-two years, I knew how to read different stares. If Jolene wasn't into me, this woman would be sucking every one of my toes before she got to my cunt.

She whispered to Jolene loud enough so I could hear, "Once you go Brown in bed, you won't frown until you're dead." I didn't expect what happened to unfold right in front of me. Jolene took a step back, distancing herself from the woman. She looked her dead in the eyes, her hand on the woman's shoulder. In a tone I hadn't yet heard from her repertoire of expressions, she said, "You can't say that, Sher. That's fucking inappropriate."

"It's cool, Jolene," I said, smiling because of the way Sher's face fell despite it being obvious that she'd had plenty of work done. I was too tired to deal with the issue. I mean, if anything, I knew I'd make Jolene feel *very* good in bed, but that was beside the point, of course.

Sher squared her shoulders, her mouth agape. She paused and thought for a second. "You're right, Jo. I'm sorry."

Jolene shook her head, watching Sher walk away towards Hawaiian Shirt. He was side-eyeing us closely.

"I'm so sorry about that," said Jolene, her fingers clenched in each hand.

"Jolene. Look at me. I'm good." I laughed. "Are you okay?"

"I'm fine. I'm really glad you're here." She held my hand briefly. I could see she was drained.

"Same. It is sort of funny . . . what Sher said."

Jolene's smiles were constantly changing. The one she had when she looked at me then was naughty, pulling up from one side before resting into a stern pout.

"Well, she can't get away with saying it. Not here."

I felt my existence and it was large, but I knew that in the café I was still a speck on the wall. I put my hand on Jolene's shoulder to show her that all was indeed fine.

"I should really head out," I said. "Plus, I'm sure you have a lot going on."

"Are you sure?"

I nodded.

"Are you okay to drive? Did you have enough to eat?"

I smiled, raising an eyebrow. Did she really care?

"I just want to be sure you're okay. Text me so I know you're home safe," she said. We were face-to-face, looking in each other's eyes, playing an unintentional game of Who Will Blink First. She lost, because she looked at my lips and then gulped.

"Have a good night, Jolene," I said. And she touched my arm, before I walked away towards the exit feeling her gaze on me the whole time.

31

Dr. Thelma Hermin Hesse had said in one of her videos to breathe in through your nose and out through your mouth. To not let life get the better of us, and that the peace we needed was inside ourselves. The peace I needed, though, was not inside anything, and the peace we all needed could be solved with some proper monies and social security. But I'm not an economist, and Dr. Thelma Hermin Hesse was probably not a real doctor.

I stood outside our front door, suddenly wishing I was back at the fundraiser, and took a few breaths in and then out. Downstairs, Phil Collins was on loud. "Against All Odds" must've been on repeat. Seeing me, Amma raised her voice as much as she could above the music. "I can't live like this," she said. "I can't live like this. Take me now. End my misery!"

I am not a saint and I am not a sinner. Casually, I walked to Amma's mattress, grabbed the pillow beside her, and stuffed it in her face, pushing it deeper until she started to choke. Then I held it three seconds longer before throwing it on the floor.

"What the hell are you doing?" she gasped.

"Get up!" I carried her, then forced her onto her feet,

grabbing her hands. I pushed her up the stairs and she slipped and fell on her knees, so I dragged her a few steps before she stood up on her own, trying to keep her balance. She took one step, two steps, then three. When I opened the front door the chill night air raised goosebumps on my skin as it blew on my sweat.

"This is the world you've been hiding from. See? It's not so bad." Hell was not a pit of fire. It was here, in the city, on the driveway, in my heart. I handed Amma a cigarette. Though she quit smoking years ago she put it in her mouth. I lit it, looking in her eyes for a second, then concentrating on the tip of her smoke. When she took a deep breath in, tears fell from her face, and she sniffled between every drag, shaking. Of course I couldn't look. We smoked in silence until she was halfway through her cigarette.

"I want to go inside," she said reluctantly. I took a few more drags and stubbed it out in the water bottle I kept on the side of the step for roaches and cigarette butts. Then I kissed Amma's forehead. Deep breath in through the nose. I carried my mother back downstairs.

32

I woke up to missed calls from Jolene. She had sent me a message shortly after I left the café: *After they turned the lights off at 10, the power actually went out!*

Then another when she got home: *Sorry we didn't get to speak much. Maybe it was a stupid idea to invite you before we could actually talk. I'd like to see you again? x*

And finally a message in the morning: *I hope you got home safe xx*

33

Once, I had a girlfriend who climaxed really loud and it was getting embarrassing. I had to tell my parents she was my best friend and that when she came over and slept in my bedroom, she had nightmares that she was in a screaming competition. The winner of course screamed the loudest. Appa had advised that maybe my friend ought to drink some warm milk with mushed bananas and a sprinkling of cinnamon at night. He even made it for her the few times she came over. Amma argued that I was probably a bit gay. (She didn't always buy into my lies.) My parents loved each other, but they disagreed on a lot of things.

Amma first went selectively paralyzed when her dad died six years ago. She was silent and motionless, lost in a dark place. We not only lost Amma as a person but ten months of her usual income. That was when they could no longer afford our little two-bedroom home and settled for renting out what was once our own basement. My parents' royal landlords slept above them—their footsteps a constant reminder of what they'd had—in the room where they used to sleep. As any young adult would, I knew it was time for me to fly the coop and not just because I was bringing people over and doing disgusting things to them under my parents' roof. But because the basement was dingy even as far as basements went, and there was only one bedroom.

Someone wrote about me on the internet and said, *Damani Krishanthan is a rowdy loose Tamil girl. She is a disgrace to her parents. She won't even stay home and help them out financially. She is the biggest bitch out there and she eats pussy.*

I swear to God people write shit on the internet about folks they haven't even spoken to. Though actually, I knew who wrote the defamation on me—it was this girl who lived on our street with her mother. She was clearly insane, but everyone's got problems. I was so close to going over and scaring them, but I knew the difference between right and wrong, even if that bitch clearly didn't. Good guys finish last? No. Nice people get fucked over. I wrote a letter to the mayor instead. Told her people in our neighborhood need better services.

When I moved out I lived with four other people. Once, and only once, three of us had a threesome. I spread blankets on the living-room floor, lit candles, and rolled a fat joint. They both said it was the best time they ever had. I thought it was okay. Since gaining some tone and muscle, as well as a better grasp of how much of my own body hair I was comfortable with, I wished I could meet all my former lovers again. We'd have an even better time. But those ships had long sailed; and anyway I knew that even before I was better, I'd still been an unforgettable fuck.

"Are you my driver?" A woman knocked on my window and I jumped in my seat. I'd nearly forgotten I was waiting in my car.

"What's your name?"

"No, I'm supposed to ask you. Never mind. I have no time." She sat in the front, beside me. That was nice. "You don't creep me out. Can you drive a little faster than normal, please?"

"Absolutely."

I revved for no reason other than to convince her this was going to be speedy. I drove as fast as I could to a veterinary clinic, maybe crossing one red light. When we arrived she said, "Can you please wait. I'll pay you extra." I waited for thirty-three minutes. For two of those minutes I thought about my old housemates. For three of them I thought about the day Toni called me to say there was shit about me on the internet. For the rest, I thought about Jolene.

The woman came back in, crying. Her dog Billy had just died on the vet's table. Billy had found her collection of elastic hair bands and had an open buffet. The vets couldn't save him and he suffocated to death. She felt comfortable enough to fall on my shoulder and cry.

"I loved him more than I love God," she said.

I stroked her hair, then drove her home.

34

How many times did I say I was tired in a given day? I had a ping and another and some more, and then gave myself a headache working out how much more money I needed to pay X, Y, and Z, without forgetting T, U, V, and W. These days, if you can find a part of the city that is quiet, without a person made homeless or a demonstration, where everyone looks as if they're having a good time, you can call yourself lucky.

I pulled my car up to the side of the road near a park downtown. Now, I wasn't following Jolene—it's a big city and stalking someone you just met could be a job in itself. But I guess some things are meant to happen. I dropped off the latest passenger of the day—Seema (4.8 stars)—and realized I was on the same street as the Mademoiselle Ethiopia Café. And so was Jolene.

I checked my teeth quickly in the mirror and hit the break button on RideShare before climbing out of my car. I walked nonchalantly towards her. She was deep in conversation with Kat, the two of them clad in Lycra sets. Jolene's was navy blue. She saw me and then smiled. I may have melted a bit.

"I think I manifested this," she said, kissing me lightly

on the cheek before looking me in the eyes. I know she noticed how I blushed. "Kat, you remember Damani?"

Standing beside Kat, Jolene looked different. An apricot-colored yoga mat was squished under her arm and her skin looked as though she had already come back from a workout—glossy yet dry. Kat sipped from her water bottle, nodding her head.

"Namaste, yogi. Of course I remember! Did Jo tell you about my award-winning yoga class? Are you here to join?"

"Only taking a break from work, maybe next time."

"But you can take a break anytime, right?" asked Jolene.

"Yeah, but—"

"To independent entrepreneurs! Look at us all," cheered Kat.

It was 1:56 in the afternoon and Jolene clearly hadn't been to work yet, unless midday yoga was part of her job description. I smiled, and Kat winked at Jolene, calling over her shoulder that it was nice to see me again.

"Do you think it would make her nervous if I—"

"Actually joined her class? Oh my God, yes! It would."

"Because she assumes I was born in child pose?"

"Born in bow with prayer beads in your mouth."

"Om sri something om."

"Exactly." Jolene's laugh was deep before it went an octave higher and she bit her lip when she saw me half-smiling. A group of four people approached her with mats under their arms and bags slung on their backs. One touched her gently from behind. I watched as they all took turns air-kissing Jolene's cheeks. Standing in frame, they were a photographer's dream. Diversity? Tick, tick, and tick, Jolene was a worldly chick. Maybe she could not only afford five-star events, but she'd also take the time to understand who I was, from the deepest to the shallowest parts of me.

"Yesterday was fab," said a woman who had a single purple roller in her hair.

"Those cops got an earful," said another friend, and they all laughed.

"Don't even get me started," said Jolene, and I wondered what she would have said if she had started.

"Girl, you're coming over tonight, right? I'm making maqluba."

Jolene's eyes rolled to the back of her head. "I'll so be there," she said, regaining her composure.

Her friends walked away towards Kat, who was now walking around a circle of mats with a singing bowl. Jolene watched them contentedly. Eventually, she looked down at her feet, remembering that I was still there in front of her. Her eyes slowly lifted up towards mine. She swallowed and brushed my arm, picking up from her touch the night before. "You didn't return my calls or messages. Did I say something?" she asked.

"No, not at all. I've been busy driving. I try not to use my phone unless I'm logged on, you know. I was tired last night."

"Right. Of course."

"You were hosting and I didn't want to intrude."

"You? Intrude? Not at all. I liked having you there."

"It was nice seeing you in action."

"Don't move. You've got something . . . Hang on." In one gentle stroke she touched just under my nose, dragged her finger down over my lips, looking into my eyes as she did it. She showed me her finger.

"An ant?"

"Who would've thought."

"On my face?"

"They're good luck, you know."

"Says who?"

"Says me."

Now Jolene felt like she couldn't be more than an inch away. Ants really are the luckiest of all supposed lucky charms.

"I gotta go," I said.

Jolene's eye contact nearly had me forgetting my name. She blinked and then studied her forearm, the ant somewhere on her skin. She said, "Thanks for finding me," before reaching over and squeezing my arm, holding on for slightly too long. I could feel her touch there an hour later. *That* was the power Jolene had.

35

"The thing about the fight for anti-racism is, as long as there is capitalism there will be racial exploitation. My freedom here doesn't mean freedom for someone else back home, you know what I'm saying?"

"Next up!"

"It's your turn, aunty. You said all this the last time I saw you, by the way." I was speaking to a woman probably in her late fifties, who was waiting in line; she showed up regularly at Doo Wop with the countless others who stared hopefully at the job boards. I'd also seen her sitting in two CV workshops, scribbling in a gray notebook, taking what seemed to be very precise notes. Neither were able to land her a job.

"I've been saying all of this since 1979. You don't have followers, do you?" she asked as she walked towards a table and out of the queue.

"I hope not."

"Good. Kids these days are losing sight with all of that nonsense," she shouted while taking a bag from the table set out under the Survival Packs banner at Doo Wop that was made with an old bedsheet, strips of used flannels, and felt.

I flashed her a peace sign (or is it V for victory?) and walked through the bar noticing that the queue for food and household items was getting longer each week; it meandered nearly from the front hall to the bend of the bar. Bob Marley and the Wailers sang about not worrying about a thing, but I had no energy to get in the groove even with the reggae rhythm chop pulling me to peel off that layer of negativity that clothed me. The two little lovebirds were seated at a table with papers in front of them, under a string of rainbow fairy lights. I had my switchblade in my back pocket and pulled it out, gripping the wood handle. I flicked it open. Creeping slowly from behind, I held the knife out and in front of Stephanie when I was close enough. All she saw was my wrist, a few inches of my arm, and my hand holding the shiny blade.

"Give me all your money," I whispered in her ear.

"What the—? Fucking hell, Damani! Don't do that again!" She slapped my arm, causing her bangles to jingle.

"You still logged on?" asked Shereef.

"Nah. Heading home."

"They have live reggae on tonight," said Steph, still holding her neck with her right hand.

"Don't you ever sleep?"

"I start late tomorrow. Oh! Tell me! Tell me! Toni says you're cunt-struck—"

"What? I could have pussy and cocks lining up outside my front door, if I wanted."

Stephanie laughed. Shereef shook his head to rid himself of the image.

"So, this is *actually* important. We've got a solid group going," he said.

"Work stuff? You're logged off."

"This is life stuff." Shereef rubbed Stephanie's leg. She rolled her eyes and brushed his hand off. "We don't just want fair wages," Shereef continued.

"We don't?"

"Come on! They'll put us on contracts with a low hourly rate with benefits and still make money off of us."

"Private healthcare is expensive," I said.

"Private school is too," added Steph.

"Seriously. We're more than just drivers. You have a degree. People have other skills."

"So, I'll get paid more if I go on about what I remember of Michel Foucault? Here's an extra twenty bucks, kid!" I banged the table.

"What? No. Listen. We *are* the company. The entire app should be all of ours." Shereef's eyes were so dark they made me love mine too. He had these pretty lashes, and his dimples topped off all the charm in his face. "She's not listening," he said to Stephanie, frustrated. "Damani, come on!" he groaned.

"So tell me about the white girl." Stephanie changed the subject, leaning closer across the table.

"It doesn't matter that she's white," snapped Shereef.

"*Rich* white girl," Stephanie snapped back. "Did she wear cashmere?" She raised her eyebrows.

"She wore a dress."

"Take pics of her outfits for me. I want to see what she's about."

"I don't know if I'll see her again. It was kind of a weird date at this fundraiser thing? Anyway, I'd have to tell her to take her shoes off at my house, maybe. I'd have to explain stuff. I'm too tired for that."

"Is she an ally?" asked Steph.

"Seems so. She could be—"

"We need comrades, not just allies," interrupted Shereef.

"What's her circle like?"

"She's got a mixed crew."

"Would they hang out here?"

"They'd write reviews, maybe. Come for the ambiance, the experience. I don't know. They seem alright."

"The ambiance?" Shereef laughed.

"She could hang here, I guess. I didn't really speak to her much at the event, to be fair."

"Really? So it wasn't a *date* date," Stephanie asked, straightening the pile of paper in front of her. I shrugged my shoulders as I watched other people come in, drinks in hand. "Maybe give her a call. Actually have a conversation."

"Maybe."

"If she was anything in your car right now, what would she be?" asked Shereef because sometimes that's how we made the most sense to each other.

I didn't have to think long; I said, "She'd be my seat belt."

"Interesting."

"You think?"

"As long as she makes you feel good, that's promising," reassured Shereef.

"Wait, what am I in your car?" Stephanie asked him.

"My engine." He smiled. Steph rolled her eyes again, this time trying very hard not to blush.

"Oh, I forgot to tell you. We picked up Pa's Deviled Beef sandwiches from Hot Kitchen," she said reluctantly.

"And?"

"They didn't taste the same." Her eyes turned glossy. "I'm sorry," she said. I leaned forward and kissed her cheek before standing up.

"Bet they didn't. See you two later. I have to go."

"You don't want a drink? Some food?"

"I'm good."

I walked out of Doo Wop and felt the world again, heavy on my shoulders. Instead of opening my car door, I opened my trunk, eyeing all the items I had hidden, wondering what it would feel like to drown myself in the bucket. Just for a few seconds, for a few days. I grabbed a bottle of water instead and poured it on my face. It was cool and fresh on my tired skin.

36

The spring in my mattress hit my side. I heard
Amma snoring while the television hummed drivel, and
I got up to switch it off. Her body was a lump under her
shroud, moving up and down gently with each nasal
breath. At Appa's funeral I thought I saw his toes move. I
thought I saw his lips try so desperately to speak the last
words I'd ever hear, but they would forever be unknown
to me. I often wonder what he may have said. Maybe he
would've told me my mother would be an extra weight
not worth carrying. I stepped on the side table to look
out the window and saw the patch of grass in the backyard where we used to have picnics. Appa would plant
his seedlings into the raised beds he'd made, and I lay on
the lawn reading books by Judy Blume. I thought, Well,
at least Appa wasn't shot, but that didn't sit right because
I knew damn well his life had been taken. How does one
prove that sort of thing? Who could I speak to for that
sort of justice? I worked it out. If Appa had been paid five
dollars more every hour, that would have been ten hours
of work less each week, forty hours less a month.

My phone buzzed. It was Jolene. *I think we need an
escape. Let's go to the beach. Tomorrow? Pick me up as*

early as you can? I had to work but I could change my hours. I drove when I had to and sometimes when I wanted to. Jolene was thinking of me and clearly couldn't sleep either. I'd have to ask Shereef to pick up Mrs. P. for her bingo runs and I'd have to tell Mrs. P. it would be Shereef picking her up. The rest of my day involved random pings. I closed my eyes and heard water and seagulls in the sky. The spring pierced sharp in my side and I let it. My phone lit up.

"Hello?"

"Hey."

"Hi."

"I just messaged you."

"Yeah," I laughed. "It's not tomorrow yet, is it?"

"Technically it is. It's twelve seventeen."

"Right. It is."

"Are you okay?"

"What do you mean?"

"I just got the sense something is off, and I know it sounds crazy, but I don't know. Maybe I shouldn't have called."

"No, no. It's cool. Yeah, all is well." In my throat there was a lump, and I hoped she hadn't heard me trying so hard to swallow it.

"Okay. I'm here if you want to talk. I know, we just met, but, yeah."

". . . What are you wearing?"

"Really?" she laughed.

"I mean, it's humid tonight."

"I've got on a T-shirt, and . . . I'm trying to think of something unsexy while I'm fully naked in bed, to be honest."

I laughed. "It's all about personality these days."

"Ah, but it is."

"What do you do for work?"

"I'm a social worker. My parents help me out a bit so that I can be one and still survive. We really don't get paid enough."

"That's kind of them."

"Yeah, they're about to retire."

"Sounds like a dream."

"Yeah. I guess I'm pretty privileged. I know."

"So, where are your hands?"

Jolene laughed again. "Ask me tomorrow. You'll need some sleep if you really want to find out." Her voice, her words. She knew exactly what she was doing to me.

37

She sat in my car and made herself comfortable. Her hands smoothed over her white beach dress and I noticed her wooden thumb ring. She smelled of lavender and periwinkle. What did periwinkle smell like? Like her. Mrs. Patrice had once told me that periwinkles were called the flower of death. Something about headbands for dead children and criminals marching to their execution. But the woman who sat beside me was the flower and the entire season of spring. We had two cups of coffee in the cup holders by my gearbox. They were the most expensive cups of coffee I'd ever paid for and they didn't taste any better than Doo Wop's. Her water bottle was on the other side, in the little space on the side of the door. On the mat in front of her were her sandals, those ones with the comfy cork soles. She showed off all her toenails in their well-kept trim. In her canvas bag, which she placed comfortably beside my backpack, she said she'd brought a picnic for us, full of treats just for me. My whole body felt relaxed. I was noticing small details.

I had prepared sandwiches using the tomato chutney Appa and I had made last summer. Stephanie's mom had unripe tomatoes which she'd planted too late and which

Appa and I salvaged using my grandmother's recipe. I knew the chutney in those sandwiches would be the best Jo had ever tasted. I'd also packed some carrots and home-made protein balls, for balance.

"Do you go to the beach often?" she asked, watching me as I drove, studying my arms. I had several tattoos on display today that I usually kept covered because people in my car always had to ask about them. But I was proud of them; a couple I had inked myself using a needle, a pen, and some India ink I bought online for twenty bucks. The sun shows off all definition. Hairs, texture, muscles peeking through working limbs. I gripped the wheel and could tell she was looking at my hands, then my face, then my lips. She smiled.

"I used to go more often. Me and my roommates would have barbecues with my friends Steph and Toni."

"That sounds like fun."

"It always is. We all hung out a lot more when we were younger. This past year has been especially rough, you know, but we try."

"Yeah. I get that. You know what I like about you?"

The road was smooth. Our conversation smooth too.

"Tell me."

"You don't have to say much. It's like—I don't know—I think you're kind of special."

I looked at her because what could I have possibly said in response? What I wanted to say was, Your presence forces me to forget all my words, and my thoughts blur into a bundle, and I want this day to never end because having you sit beside me makes me feel at ease. I also wanted to say that I kinda thought she might be full of bullshit and maybe I was in a vulnerable place, but if I'm honest with myself I didn't want to even think that. What I said instead was, "It isn't all about looks, Jo."

"Absolutely. I know that."

"People are complex and have different facets to them. You can't go around trusting just anyone." She laughed and plugged her phone in my aux. The car behind us honked. My eyes weren't on the road.

"You're going to love this," she said, explaining that the band she was playing were from Morocco—they were from Mali. She said they sang in Arabic—they sang in Tamashek, but everyone makes mistakes and she had good taste in music. I didn't tell her I knew the band; I wanted her to feel she was blowing my mind, and she was, but not in the way she perhaps intended. She asked if I'd heard any Kris Kristofferson, then she played a song she promised I'd love.

"My turn," I said after some time. The traffic light was red and I plugged my phone in. She closed her eyes as if she was waiting to die in my car and go to heaven through sounds she'd never heard before. Scrapper Blackwell strummed his guitar with so much emotion, I thought that even if Jolene had listened to him before, this would be her first time listening with me. She put her hand on my thigh in between the second and third verses. I looked at her for a second before concentrating back on the road while she caressed me with her fingers.

"There's something about you that makes me want to know more," she said, nestling in my passenger seat.

"There's something about you that makes me want to tie you up and do things to you."

I didn't mean to say that out loud, but I was weirdly a little nervous. Indulging in sexy is easy, but speaking truth to connection is not. It wasn't all about lust like Toni and Steph thought. Jolene was brand new to me. She was mythologized and we were all told she was Holy. Or at least, women like her. Of course, I didn't buy into any of that rhetoric, but there she was, sitting in my car, obsessed with me. She looked at me, flattered. Closing her legs tenderly, her hips pushed back, and I knew it felt good to grind on my seat the way she did. She took a sip of her cold and very expensive coffee, then let out a little gasp.

38

The blanket was a deep wine cashmere, woven with soft blue and gray threads. I laid it out on a perfect spot where the sun was right above us. The water was clear and the beach was ours, except for the random dog walkers, and the retirees taking in the many years of their life on an oversized veranda. Most of the people in the city were working, of course, but there were residential neighborhoods close by. I envied whoever could live beside water. I had driven up to the lakes one night and found out that some people had one for a backyard. Literally, their backyard was a lake. If that wasn't stolen land, I don't know what is.

Jo took the treats she had packed from out of her canvas bag. Strawberries, walnuts, and chocolate almonds. How did she even know? Was she stalking me? Or was this serendipity? She had more expensive drinks that promised to make one feel cleared and cleansed. She'd brought champagne and flutes without a speck of hard water dried on the glass. I took my protein balls, carrots, and sandwiches out and put them onto our picnic spread.

"My mom has a giant rhubarb patch at our summer house. She makes the best crumble. I'll make sure there's one ready when you come over."

"When I come over?"

She smiled.

"Okay," I said. "Then I'll make rhubarb syrup. Add it to some vodka with a sprig of mint, some strawberry slices, maybe a bit of ginger."

"That sounds amazing. I think my mom would like you." Jolene tilted her head, studying my face as if I was a masterpiece. I played to her gaze. "We should definitely spend a week at my summer house. There's a lake and a tree house, some horses too. You'd have to meet my favorite, Lawrence. He's got a diamond spot and a lazy eye."

"I'd like that."

"I tell the kids I work with to plant rhubarb wherever they can. Even in a bucket. It can take years to grow but once it does, you'll be lucky."

"You could poison someone if you steeped the leaves in a tea," I said.

Jolene mumbled something with a sandwich in her hand, then looked up at me. Under the sun she was an ethereal beast; the blond hairs on her arms looked etched on her skin. I knew she wouldn't mind the hairs on my toes.

"Have you ever seen the root system of a rhubarb plant?" she asked. "It's huge. Robust. It looks like slender, long sweet potatoes. They're giant tubers. If you have a few chunks of it, you could sell it for a hundred. A little less, a little more."

"People spend that much on roots?"

"Rhubarb roots, oh, yeah."

"So instead of growing it themselves, your kids could be on the lookout for rhubarb plants. They could dig up the roots. Start a rhubarb cartel, quit school."

"I can't tell children that, but yeah, I guess they could. They should!"

"Stephanie's mom has a patch. I'll have to borrow her hoe."

Jolene smiled and in her smile was tomorrow, three months from now, and an infinity swimming in a lake by a summer house. I stood up and held her hand. I looked at her with the sun still shining on her face. She held my other hand and I wanted her inside of me, sleeping in my chest.

"Let's go," I said, leading her to the water. She took her dress off, throwing it on the sand. She ran with her red one-piece, while I was still taking my shorts and top off. Even though I loved my body, I was not used to showing it. The water was cool on my feet. Jolene moved in it with the same ease she moved about on land.

"Can you swim?" she asked.

"Not the best. But I can do this." I walked towards her, getting used to the temperature of the water. I dove down and looked for her legs, then grabbed them from under and lifted her. I put her down so she was comfortable back in the water as droplets fell from every inch of her. My hair was heavy and on my face; I flipped it back and smiled, blowing drops of water out of my mouth. I watched her looking at me while I tried to catch my breath. The water pushed towards the shore around her body illuminating the shine of every stretch mark that wrapped around her hips, glistening like coral on her skin. Under the surface, her hands moved against the current. I pushed her slightly then dipped my hair in the water and lay on my back. I heard her hands create waves, before she lay on her back too.

"My dad taught me to swim here," I told her. "Well, first at the public pool and then when I was good enough he brought us here to get better."

"Maybe one day we can all spend a day here. My dad would love your dad."

"You don't even know mine."

"But I'm sure he's lovely."

"He died six months ago."

"I'm so sorry. I didn't know." She stood up from floating, wringing her hair behind her. Her eyes were wide and looking at me intently when she apologized. Water that had been on her face fell down her lips, and she licked each drop in a single slurp.

"It's okay," I said, repositioning myself. I looked at her. Only the sun was between us, warming our skin. She was easily someone I had seen a hundred times before, but never so close in front of me.

"My dog died last year and I'm still not over losing her. I know it's not the same but—"

"Did your dog do amazing tricks?" I asked.

"He would roll, give a paw, even did a dance if you called him Elvis."

"Did he get paid? Like, did he generate an income, was he twenty-five years old and your first best friend?" She laughed. Realizing that I wasn't joking, she said, "I know it's not the same, Damani."

"It might be."

"I shouldn't have shared it like that."

"Some people have shitty dads."

"I'm sure yours wasn't."

"Is yours?"

"He's amazing. Narrow-minded, but warmer than my mom."

"Mm . . . My friend Shereef has a friend whose dad used to beat her."

"I'm so sorry to hear that."

"She bought a turtle and told it all her problems, until the turtle got conjunctivitis and died."

"Oh no."

"It gets better."

"It gets worse?"

"She cried for days. Days."

"Aw, my heart."

"A month or so later, she finds out her dad died. Overdosed in a motel somewhere."

"And?"

"She rocked up to the motel and stabbed his corpse repeatedly with her house keys."

"What the fuck?"

"I'm kidding."

"Jesus Christ, Damani!"

"She was fine. Shrugged her shoulders and moved on." Jolene's hands had been on her head, her mouth wide open. She finally centered herself.

"So . . . bringing up my dog wasn't entirely inappropriate?"

"It was terrible."

"I really am sorry."

"I'll let it slide . . . only because the drive back to the city is long, and that could be awkward."

"I could always request another driver. Go on another date."

"Oh yeah?" She grinned, coyly. A pair of seagulls flew above us, as a flock heckled on the shore fighting over a bagel. Jolene didn't shy away from any eye contact. Her eyes said everything. I looked across to watch the hungry gulls, and her eyes were still on me. I thought, Maybe I should break the silence. I sensed my frustration made her feel uneasy. I could tell Jolene about the passenger I'd had and her dog Billy. It would comfort her and we could move on. But then she reached for my hand.

"Can I ask what happened to your dad?"

"He'd worked at the Hot Kitchen downtown since we immigrated here. Spent time working at Mira's Sundries too, but Hot Kitchen was his life."

"I've been there. They have this sandwich that I loved before I became a vegetarian. It has this amazing spicy sauce—"

"Pa's Deviled Beef. That's my dad's."

"Really?"

"Yeah, he was making deviled beef for himself, and then management had a taste. The rest is history."

"He must have got a good price for that!"

"They gave him baseball tickets. I was too young to know what was going on and my dad was happy."

"So how did he pass?"

"He finished his shift one night, and then someone called. They wanted Pa's Deviled Beef sandwiches and they wanted my dad to make them because no one made them like he did. Apparently he was smiling and singing while he fried that beef, and then his heart stopped."

"Oh my God. I'm so sorry. For everything." Jolene squeezed my hand.

"It's cool."

"Is your mom okay? She's not—"

"Dead? Nah."

"It must still be really difficult."

"It's fine. My dad and I were planning to start our own food truck someday. I'm going to start saving up for it soon, but . . . yeah."

"If things are tough . . . I can . . . I could've bought the coffees."

"Hey. Jolene. It's fine. Look at me." I flexed my biceps and rubbed my stomach. "I can handle things."

She rolled her eyes. "We can *share* things." She held my hand and touched my stomach, feeling my abs before moving her hands up my body, caressing my shoulders with the tips of her fingers. She pulled me closer and wrapped her arms around my neck. She looked into my eyes, searching. When it felt as if she'd found something, she kissed me.

39

She held my bottom lip for as long as she could, sucking and licking as my tongue explored her warm mouth. I couldn't say how much time had passed. Her eyes were closed. Water jeweled on her skin, her eyes gentle and dreamy when she opened them. She smiled and I saw how she lived with her heart before anything else. The lines on her face, her pores, her speckles and freckles, a scar she had on the bottom of her chin. We walked out of the water holding hands. I let go when we reached the shore.

She had sand stuck between her toes. The wind blew through her hair, though mine flew towards her like black silk trying to strangle her. She looked up at me with her Little Miss Sweetheart grin, as if she knew exactly where the line of light was and how it would catch her face. Her canvas bag was now filled with half-eaten foods and still nearly full bottles of expensive water.

"Look at that hermit crab." She crouched down in front of it. "The world isn't that scary, is it? You don't need to hide, little thing." It seemed as though the crab looked right up at us and decided it was best to stay inside its shell. Jo reached her hand out anyway. In a perfect story, the crab would've had second thoughts. It would've peered from out of its shell and slid up into her palm. But this isn't a perfect story. It hasn't been since I started it.

"Let's go."

She stood up and I tried hard to keep my hands to myself. I had a cigarette because it was going to be another long drive, and though I knew that I'd enjoy it, my body was sore and, even though Jo made me feel worthy of her, I was still slightly on edge. I lit the cigarette, inhaled, exhaled, and watched it burn. As much as I saw her, I wondered how much of me she saw. How much did she know by the random choke of my voice? How much did she sense in our silence?

"Do you smoke cannabis every day?"

"This is tobacco."

"But you smoke cannabis?"

"Only when the day hurts. Or when I want to feel something a little more. Maybe that's most days, but I smoke less than I used to."

"Hmm." She looked around before her eyes rested on me again. From the expression on her face, I could tell she was swooning over me. It felt like the possibilities were endless with how the sky plunged into the sea right in front of us. She found something else, other than us, to talk about.

"There's so much trash everywhere."

"People don't care about the planet."

"Do you really think so?"

"I really do."

"Tell me something. What's the thing about all of this you just can't stand?"

I didn't know what the "this" she was referring to was, but I said, "There's a lot of scum out there, and people don't really see how it's all connected. It's making us all sick. Sometimes I even think I have tumors."

Jolene took in my words; I saw how she dwelled on them deeply. She said, "It really is infuriating. I don't know what to say."

Looking back, I think maybe I should've trusted my gut here—were we really seeing the world the same? Did I let too much go unsaid? But then with such warmth, she added, "Sometimes, I want to hide as much as that crab does. Sometimes, I don't want to be here. I want to do the right thing, but maybe I get it wrong. I want to disappear some days." She smoothed the ends of her hair and placed a bundle of it against her lips, brushing the tips on her skin. Her eyes looked away from me as she continued. "I want to be free when maybe I'm the most free." She choked, and I knew that choke. Hers was a different kind of pain and I knew that. She was a little broken, certainly not broke, but breaking into empty. I put the butt in a can that had found a home on the sand. We were beside my car.

"Do you ever feel lonely?" I asked.

"I think that's what it is. When I get sad, I'm just really lonely, I guess. I know the universe has a lot in store for me, but..." She laughed, embarrassed. "What about you?"

"Me? I don't know. I ... There's always people around,

but . . ." I clenched my jaw tight. "I . . . I miss my dad. I'm always exhausted. I'm made to feel like this world isn't for people like me." I gulped. Why the fuck did I say all that? Standing in front of me, she caressed my arms, moving her hands along my skin. I put my own on her shoulders, running my fingers down to her waist, caressing her skin as we connected in the silence.

"You're really special, Damani. I'm sorry you've ever felt otherwise. This world sucks most of the time, but it doesn't have to anymore. I really do feel so different when I'm with you," she said.

"You make me feel alive."

"What?"

"You make me feel good."

Her fingers traced along my arms, resting on my hips. She pulled the elastic on the top of my shorts, digging her thumbs underneath and then she pulled me closer. Her breath was raspy in my ear. Her hand found my cunt and her fingers pressed gently. The song of the water, behind us. I bit her chin, she bit my neck.

"Let's go in the car," she whispered.

40

Her legs were thrown over my shoulders; her head was leaned back against the seat. I pushed myself forwards and squeezed into the space, trying to ignore the fact that I was basically in a footwell. I didn't care, I wanted her. My lips were all over her skin. My tongue found her nipples. She groaned. I was gentle.

Men don't realize just how delicate we are down there. Start slow, caress the lips, don't hit the button. Take all the time in the world. Her hands gripped behind her for stability, making streaks on my back window. She was sour in my mouth. I licked her thighs, tasting the salt on her skin. I knew when I looked down and rested my chin that the seat beneath her had held more people, and more vomit, than would make either of us comfortable, but I quickly pushed it out of my mind when she grabbed my hair and moaned. It turned me on to see what I did to her.

"Wait, wait. There's no one here," she said between gasps, still grinding on my face. She opened the door and got out, pulling at me to follow her. She wasn't afraid of showing me how much she wanted me. She walked around to the front of my car, and bent herself over the hood, before reaching down to touch her pussy. Fuck. Of course I was falling for her. She leaned against the car, my car, with come-get-me eyes.

"Is this okay? Can I do this?" asked Jo.

I leaned towards her, wrapping my leg around her, bringing her closer with my arm, then I kissed her neck. We were naked and maybe someone was watching but I didn't think about it. Our bodies were close, and we rocked, finding each other's rhythm. She bit my neck harder and scratched at my back, but I kept going until she was limp and shuddering in my arms.

"You're fucking sexy," she whispered.

"I've got a big heart too."

She laughed. And we lay on that hood, kissing, touching, and teasing until we were ready to go again.

41

While I drove back to the city, Jo had her hand on my thigh again.

"Do you ever wish you could just drive, and drive, and drive?"

"All the time, but gas is expensive."

"The sun makes me hungry. You want anything?"

I shook my head. She reached towards the backseat. There was some rustling. She picked out a chutney sandwich I'd packed for her.

"What did you think of the chutney?" I asked.

"Oh my God, didn't you hear me while I had the sandwich on the beach? I'm sure I said it was the best I've ever had. Did you make it?"

"Maybe. Yeah. My dad did mostly, actually."

"That is really special. Thank you for sharing it with me."

"We share things, right?"

"Everything."

She took a few more bites, then shifted in her seat and asked, "Do you think I'm in shape?"

"Only you would know that."

"You're in really good shape."

"Cardio doesn't exist in my life."

"You're modest."

"This paramedic said a thing that pissed me off. Have you ever tried to build muscle? It's like eating cocaine."

"What?"

"I think you're the most beautiful woman I've ever seen."

"You say things as though you think that's what you're meant to say." She looked out the window before turning back to me. "You don't have to do that with me, I like you for you."

She was right. I didn't have to say anything. I was about to reply but my phone lit up.

Amma had sent me a message: *Where are you? I have a pain.*

"Everything okay?" asked Jolene.

42

Amma had had many pains before. Real pains, fake pains, excruciating pains that no doctor could diagnose, but which I felt through her wails in the middle of the night. She had said nightmares were the worst when you woke up in the same shithole situation you were in before bed. Amma was a dramatic feeler, and that was okay. But she managed to be incredibly dramatic when I was tired or about to get laid, again.

Jolene was my car radio. She went on about a summer in Barcelona and a night at Bible camp. To coming out when she was drunk on boxed wine and throwing up right after.

"I told my parents I liked men, but I mainly liked women. My dad said it could be a phase, a stop before gay, or that I was just like him. He hasn't come out to me, so I don't know what he meant."

"Queer-baiter."

"Basically. My mom is more rigid. I mean, she's comfortable with it all, but she is incredibly straight. She fits the mold for the most part. What about you?"

"I like people. Cunts and cocks and long walks on the beach." She made a face so I added, "I like connecting with people." I didn't get into how Appa never knew of my bisexuality, or that Amma cried for thirty days when she saw me kissing a girl. She had stopped speaking to me too. When Appa was working overtime one night, I locked the television programming on lesbian porn. Amma called me, crying, and apologized. She had said, "Fine, fine. Do whatever you want, Damani. Just stop the boobies and poonies. What are these women doing?"

The day was long, and a fizz rose up in my chest. I had realized that Amma hadn't called me all morning. Her texts weren't followed by a string of more texts and calls like they usually were. Jolene went on talking and I tried my best to listen. She said on Mondays she had spin class at seven p.m., on Tuesday mornings she used to do Bikram yoga, but thank God she didn't get involved in that shit anymore. She did Ashtanga yoga now, at six p.m., and Kat's sessions in the afternoons whenever she could. On Wednesdays she helped make dinner at a homeless shelter. On Thursdays she held an after-school club for kids at the school nearby her office; Fridays she had a large smoothie with extra flax seeds at Carly's Fruit Bob because by Friday, a cleanse was the best way to start the weekend, she said. Saturday evening was book-club night at the Mademoiselle Ethiopia Café, Sunday morning she dropped off the surplus of baked goods from the café to the community center, and Sunday night she went for a jog at the track by her house.

By the time she'd told me all of this, I had turned down my street.

"I think some of the young people I work with live around here," she said, looking out the window as I drove through my neighborhood. "What happened to your street sign?"

"Teenagers, probably," I lied, pulling into our drive. "I just have to check up on my ma and then I'm all yours. Give me a sec."

"Hang on," she said, reaching around and pulling something out of her bag. "Before I forget, I brought something for you. I wasn't sure when to give it to you." I looked at the time and then she handed me a bag. Delicately placed inside it was a bottle of wine, a bath bomb, and a bag of chocolate almonds. Almost all the stress of the drive dissipated.

When I moved to the basement after Appa died, I didn't want to bring anyone over, especially because Amma was practically dying herself, and I didn't want to be close to anyone. Then I went through a few weeks of wanting to do nasty things to everyone because in the few hours I frolicked naked with a body, I felt something before I felt nothing again.

"Come with me. Just for a bit. You'll give my ma something else to think about." I noticed the look on Jolene's face, but I couldn't work out what it was. "It doesn't mean we're getting married, don't worry. You can stay in the car if you want."

Downstairs, Amma was under her covers on the couch. The place smelled of cold rub and crackers. I didn't remember leaving the box of crackers out. I pulled the cover from Amma's face.

"Hey, Ma, did you walk to the kitchen today?"

"No. Who is she?"

Jolene's eyes widened. Her body was tense. She held herself without holding on to anything.

"Hi. I'm Jolene."

"I don't understand you. Who is she?"

"This is a woman I just met and already slept with. Did you eat your dinner?"

"She looks like she's not from here."

"Did you eat, Ma?"

"It hurts, D. I don't want to watch any more movies. I can't live like this. Just let me go, please." I knelt down beside her and put the bag Jolene had given me on the floor.

"Are you seriously going to do this right now?"

"I'm so sad, mahal."

I opened the gift bag and took out the bath bomb. "Look. You put this in the bathtub and it explodes into bubbles. I can pour you a glass of wine. It's the good stuff that won't give you a headache. You can put your feet up and I'll read you something Appa had on his shelf." I kept the chocolate almonds in the bag. Those were mine. "I'm going to drop my friend home and then I'll be back. The feeling will pass. Tomorrow we'll walk to the park if you can."

"Go away, Damani."

I had kept the bottle of sleeping pills away from Amma but every now and then, I gave her one. That night, she needed two. I brought her the pills and a glass of water, and then I kissed her head.

"Ready?" I asked Jolene, noticing that she'd folded one of Amma's blankets. Her face was different, and I hoped it wasn't because she saw how I lived. It was the face of a baby gibbon or a kitten or something else you'd want to hold tight all night. Her mouth opened but she didn't make a sound. I led her up the stairs and back outside and realized she had, in fact, taken off her shoes.

43

We didn't say a word to each other in the car, but she put her hand on my knee. She looked at me, asking if it was okay. Her hand was warm. She ran it up my thigh, then back down to my knee in comforting strokes that tingled in all the right places.

I parked the car outside of her place. It was late and I knew that even if she asked, I wouldn't go inside. I turned off the engine sensing her eyes studied my every move. The car was warm and the heat between us created a foggy haze even though the evening was clear.

"I'm not going to open your door," I said. Her seat belt was already snapped off, her body turned towards me.

"I would never even ask," she said studying my mouth. Looking at my rear-view I noticed a sliver of dried blood on my bottom lip. Feigning embarrassment, she said, "Sorry about that," while reaching to scratch her ankle. I could tell she was thinking, thoughtfully working out how best to say what was on her mind. "Your mom seems pretty nice."

"I wouldn't say I have a type, Jolene, but if I did, it wouldn't be you," I blurted, my hands tight on the wheel. I waited for a few seconds before looking at her reaction.

She smiled, blinking slowly. "Well, I don't like cat-egorizing people, either. I guess I'm flattered to be here beside you." Then she cleared her throat and added, "But you know what they say, once you go Brown . . ." Her eyes rolled in perfect half circles and she shivered as though her words contaminated her blood.

"You're terrible!" I teased. We were both smiling. She looked at her hands before looking up at me. Shereef's spray was pungent now and rising from the upholstery on my backseat, acidic and lemony fresh.

"You know, if you ever need some space, you're always welcome at mine. Even as a friend or whatever, my door is always open."

"Sex on the first date and now you're asking me to move in with you?"

Jolene laughed, more than I thought she would. "I'm serious," she said.

I nodded, still processing the entire day.

"And anyway, we're women of the twenty-first cen-tury." She beamed. "We can do whatever we want." I stared at my wheel before tapping it with my fingers. The sound was distinct, my rhythm doubling in speed. "I'm trying really hard not to suggest we plan a vacation," she confessed.

"Sorry, what?"

"I have a friend who owns a villa in Italy. We could go to Naples, visit a vineyard, go to the beach."

"We just came from the beach."

"That is true."

"Plus, I can't be away for too long."

"My summer house, then. We're so going to my summer house. And you can leave whenever you want. Your mom is more than welcome too. There's a guest room, and you can have the whole house if it's free."

"Oh yeah?"

"For sure. This city is depressing and I have a lot of fun with you."

I popped the hood and got out of my car for some air. I lifted it open and looked around, toying with bits not having a clue of what I was doing. Keep cool, breathe. She couldn't see me. Carefully putting the hood down, I walked around to Jolene's side and opened her door. I held my hand out for her.

"Really?" She laughed.

"On my off hours I offer special services." I knew she wasn't actually the sort of woman interested in having her door opened. She took my hand and hung on to it. Her fingers played between mine. She shut the door and leaned against the car.

"I know that I'll never truly understand what it's like for—"

"Do you have a record collection?"

"I do. And I've got some wine in the fridge."

"Maybe, show me another time?" I whispered in her ear, seeing the hairs on her neck stand.

"Mmm. Okay. I, uh . . . normally don't have sex on the first date, by the way." She grinned.

"I don't believe you, Jolene."

She pulled me closer.

"Besides, it was our second." My body collapsed against hers and I felt freer than I had in a long time. Our noses touched. Her hand found the back of my head and dug through my hair, her fingers caressing my scalp. She touched me and stroked me. I wanted to bite her again. I was wet and in the summer's gentle breeze I could feel just how moist my pussy was safe in my underwear.

"You're definitely a Scorpio," she whispered.

She pulled me closer and moved an inch forward to kiss me. I leaned my head back, so she kissed my chin instead. Her hands found their way along my arms and I wanted to ask if she'd noticed how much I lift but I knew that would be vain. This wasn't the time. Her lips pressed along my neck, her breath warm on my skin. I bit her behind her ear and gripped her closer to me by her waist. I kissed her cheek. I pulled back even though I didn't want to. We took a second to catch our breath.

"You're incredible, Damani."

I watched her watch me as she pinched and pulled her bottom lip. Then she gathered her belongings. I touched her shoulder as she stood in front of me, smiling. "Good night, Jo."

By the way she looked at me, with that soft dewy expression, I knew she wanted me to kiss her cheek again. "Good night, Damani," she finally said before walking towards her house, nearly stumbling over her own foot. She styled it out with a laugh, waved, and hugged her body with her bags in her hands. Just as she got to her door, she turned around to say, "Hey! We got this." I waited until she was inside and her lights were switched on. I waited a bit longer, wondering what she was doing. Then I realized I'd better drive away before I did the wrong thing and knocked on her door.

44

I had made Amma a full breakfast before I left home. Bombay toast, a fried egg, and some frozen strawberries I cut up and mixed with sugar and chili pepper. I squeezed fresh orange juice for her with my bare hands. She didn't have a bite or a sip of anything so I knew come lunchtime she might have more of an attitude. I was standing outside my car with a cup of coffee I got for two dollars at Doo Wop, giving myself a little break before what I hoped would be a ping-after-ping sort of day.

"What do you mean, I can't get on? I have an exam this morning!"

"You think I care? You need to pay the right fare like everyone else."

A young woman stood on the steps of the bus while other passengers walked in. I had been her before. Late for school, late for work, with not enough money to get on the bus. The driver was only doing his job but he clearly cared too much about the wrong rules. I walked towards the bus.

"Here." I handed the girl twenty bucks. "Sorry, I thought I gave this to you already, sis."

"What? Are you sure? Thank you." I put the actual bus

fare in the driver's collection box, looking into a world I once knew so well. I was reminded that in my car I am safe. I was doing better than I had been, even if I wasn't. The young woman gave me a hug, then gave the driver the finger.

"Get off my bus," he said to me.

I leaned towards him, smirking. It was a sunny morning and I could still taste Jolene's lips. "Sometimes it helps to masturbate," I said to him before jumping off. "The transport company doesn't give a fuck about you."

45

My first passenger (after Mrs. Patrice) walked towards my car. When she opened the door I said, "Morning! The sun is gorgeous today." Because it was.

"I'm on my way to the radiologist. Can you do me a favor and not talk to me?"

I dropped her off, respecting her wishes. Her ride was a solid twenty bucks even though I knew a few months back, it would've been in the mid-thirties. She didn't tip me either. Then my phone pinged. Passenger number 3, Shiv (4.7 stars).

"Morning. You nice and comfy back there?"

"You know where you're going, right?"

"Oh, yeah. It tells me on the screen. I know the whole city inside out, anyway."

"Just keep your eyes on the road."

"Don't worry about a thing. Enjoy the ride."

"You kids think you know everything. But what you don't realize is how we can see your stress in your shoulders. You keep it in your shoulders, did you know that?"

"My shoulders are fine. I do get an ache every now and then because of the driving. You a doctor?"

"Have you heard of reiki? You use vitamin D? Moringa? I host retreats in Bali. Are you interested?"

"Absolutely not."

"Of course not. You don't look like an influencer."

"Do you do Bikram yoga?"

"Excuse me? I'm offended you'd even ask."

Reiki Master's ride was $13.27 with a dollar tip, and he was now safe at his destination. My phone pinged again and then again. I didn't have to wait long between pings that day and most of my journeys were away from the protests. Usually when it was sunny, people enjoyed walking or cycling or lying on the grass. There were passengers 4 and 5, and 6 and 7, and by then three of them had tipped me more than $2. Passenger number 7 (4.9 stars) said what many say: that drivers have insight like no one else in the country. He then asked me to pick seven numbers for the weekly lotto. His ride was only $7.30, zero in tips.

After him there was passenger 8, a Roxy (3.3 stars) whose big fat baby threw up on my seat, then had a runny nosebleed. A melody of "Oh my God, I'm so sorry" came from Roxy and my harmony of "It's okays" made our song complete. I dropped her and the baby at a health clinic, $14.35 with a $10 tip, drove a bit and found a place to park. Shereef's concoction had worked well with annoying Kenny's soda, but blood and vomit were thicker. I sprayed, soaked, and blotted the mess away, grateful I'd never had to clean up any cum and that Shereef's spray was the best I'd tried yet. After I'd waited an hour, the vomit smell was faint. I got another ping and then another. Passengers 9 and 10, then 11, got in the car.

"I don't believe you drivers should exist, but I missed my bus."

"Well, here I am, ready to get you to where you need to be, on time and safe, my friend."

Passenger 11 was a Claire (3.9 stars) who rolled her eyes and I still smiled; a smile that had been plastered on my face all day despite all the unpaid mileage. That sort of giddiness felt like a crime.

46

It would be dark soon and I wasn't sure if I had it in me to work that night. In one of her videos, Dr. Thelma Hermin Hesse had said that it was important to take the time we needed for ourselves so we didn't burn out like a withered flame. Behind her was Mount Kīlauea rupturing in rage. No one was actually obligated to do anything, she added. I knew that was irresponsible of her to say and my bank balance proved it, but I still watched the whole video, mesmerized by magma and technology.

I was parked outside a condominium in the business district. Suits walked home and drove by in shiny expensive cars that were an obnoxious flaunting of unnecessary metal in a game of look-whose-dick-is-bigger. This city was penis obsessed. Driven by the phallus, all for the phallus, worshiping the phallus, or at least worshiping themselves. Driving through this area I wore my shades.

There had been a large demonstration for anti-racism that afternoon, the epicenter a few blocks away. Luckily, I knew all the back roads to avoid the traffic. I was waiting for an Anthony (4.8 stars) who seemed not to care that I was sitting outside for fifteen minutes already with the meter ticking (25 percent to RideShare). Maybe he was hiding from the crowd that gathered by Carly's Fruit Bob. There were two types of people in this area: those that floated on by and were made of money, ready for a night of drinking it all away, and then the rest of us. In front of me, standing a few feet away, was a gang of superheroes who I knew had glossy pictures on their social media that made their lives look better than they were in reality. (How did people have such amazing cameras on their phones? The sorcery is beyond me.) There was the classic glass of wine in the foreground, vineyard in the back—snap. Then a casual Saturday hike—snap. A look at all the vacations I take and how my legs dangle out in front of me on a yacht/beach—snap. And of course, but only recently, a look at all the protests I've been to, my friends make up the rainbow—snap. Surely there was a Martin Luther King Jr. quote with a picture of him where his eyes were warm and gentle—snap—followed by an assortment of look at what amazing dinners I've had—snap. I couldn't be bothered to shout anything out of my window. I closed my eyes, seeing the waves, Jo's body against mine, her lips mouthing just how incredible I am. I imagined what it would be like waking up beside her in her bed. The sunlight coming in through her gossamer-thin drapes, warming my well-rested eyes. The song of the birds welcoming me. She'd roll over and say, "Let's order pancakes, even though there's fruit and yogurt in the fridge." And then I wondered if Jolene knew any of those people standing across from me.

Anthony opened my door, nearly pulling the entire handle off.

"Here's twenty bucks. Thanks for waiting."

My phone buzzed as I reached for the money. My hands touched Anthony's and we looked each other in the eye. The silence was loud before he said, "Oh, sorry."

Shereef had messaged me: *Some drivers are getting less than 40% of their usual fare rate. Don't spend your money too fast. We're setting up a stand in the park tonight. You coming?* Anthony was on his phone already, too busy to even care that I still hadn't moved the car. I thought, maybe I could get something nice for Jolene. Nothing forced, and only if I found something naturally.

"I lost a lot of passengers waiting for you. I could've made more than twenty in cash while I sat waiting here like a monkey. Give me more money or get out of my car." I wouldn't have made that much, and I wasn't waiting for *that* long, but something came over me. Anthony was eyeing me from my rear-view, holding my stare.

He moved his phone from his mouth and smirked. "If you're ever looking for a real job and have experience working with numbers, give me a call. We need people that look like you, too." He handed me a ten along with his business card. As I started the ignition, my phone buzzed again, but it wasn't another ping waiting in line and it wasn't even Amma.

It was Jolene: *Thinking of you, Damani.*

Let me see you soon. x

47

Amma followed Toni's Pilates class as it played on the screen. She did four minutes while remaining sitting on the couch. Better than nothing. I had cooked tinned mackerel in tomato sauce with onions, chilies, and loads of garlic. I buttered some toast.

"Smells good, D."

"Here." I passed her a plate and turned the screen off. If I'd had a little more cash to play with, I would've prepared salmon seared in a pan with butter and maybe some sage. Would that even work? I'd try some pepper, salt, and lemon, maybe, because that's what they suggest on those cooking shows. Appa would have done salmon and tamarind with thinly sliced onions. That makes more sense to me. They say that fish goes good with lemon and Appa taught me just how perfect lemons can be in most dishes, though he actually preferred limes. Salmon is a big fish and expensive. Maybe it had feelings because it was that big. This one time when I took a bite of the coral flesh, in the second I closed my eyes I had scales and jumped ten feet high from the salty ocean water. When I landed, I was somewhere else, missing narwhals and leatherback turtles while stuck in a cage rubbing against other salmon, seeing chunks of my body fall off my skin as sea lice ate me alive. Maybe I should stop eating salmon. Maybe it's a crime.

"Stephanie came over today. She painted my nails. She brought banana bread she baked, too."

"She ask you to make milk hoppers for her?"

"Stephanie doesn't give just to receive."

"Of course, Ma. But she loves your hoppers."

"She asked me to go for a walk with her."

"You should go," I said.

"Maybe. Where is that girl that came here? She's different."

"She's cool."

"She's not scared of you?"

"Why would she be scared of me?"

Amma shrugged.

"You like the mackerel?" I asked.

"Did you catch it?"

"I'm glad you're feeling better."

"I'm trying."

"I know, Ma. We both are."

48

If Jolene was anything, she was the sun. Perfect at a distance, but up close, she could hurt my skin. I didn't have the time or energy to think about what she and I could be together, and how that could work. But I felt something tug at my conscience. It bothered me that I didn't even know her surname yet, but I was also happy she didn't tell me. You could do a lot with someone's full name these days; I don't know why people share theirs so widely. Besides, we only went out a couple of times. It was fine. I didn't need to obsess about whatever was churning in my gut. I shifted perspective and focused on something else. I wanted to add more face-pulls to my workout so my back had tributaries of definition. I had watched another of Dr. Thelma Hermin Hesse's videos earlier in the day while I waited for a ping. "Don't waste time you don't have to give. Know your worth, and demand you receive it." Basic advice, yes, but Dr. Thelma Hermin Hesse said basic things when I needed to hear them. She had worn a purple sweater and on it was a #1.

I was on my way to pick up Mrs. Patrice from her date at a pizza parlor. Unfortunately, I wasn't able to drop her off there. She didn't often go out at night, but started to because I told her it'd be a good change from bingo mornings and afternoon lie-ins watching *Days of Our Lives* and *The Price Is Right*. Though to her credit, Mrs. Patrice spent many afternoons at the community garden, planting and directing young folks where to dig. She had invited me a few times before, and I'd planned to go with Appa, but I waited too long to arrange that. When you're gone, you're sort of gone forever.

"Mrs. P., look at you!" She wore a sequined green dress, dangling broccoli earrings—shaped like actual broccoli—and a brooch that looked like a bunch of beets. The loose and aged skin on her arms, too stubborn to slip off from her bones, glistened. In between each thin fold was a sprinkle of crushed diamonds. Along with the usual scent of her perfume, she smelled of the cocoa butter she had lathered on her arms, as well as vanilla and cranberry juice. Her hair was styled so her soft gray curls were more pronounced.

"Thank you, darling. This is Travis. Travis, this is my dear driver friend."

"Pleasure to meet you." He was shorter than Mrs. Patrice, who I realized was quite a tall woman. Amma would describe them as an "*if*" couple. Travis the short "*i*," Mrs. P. the towering "*f*." Travis was mole-ish, brutish, but soft around the edges. There was certainly something about his smile. They looked good together standing outside the pizza parlor in their finest clothes. "All right, you. I had an excellent time." He held her hand and suddenly Mrs. P. blushed and kissed his cheek.

"So how was it?" I asked, starting the engine after Travis had shut the door, waving goodbye.

"He smelled like garlic."

"What? You looked so into him."

"Just because someone has an odor doesn't mean they can't be loved. You of all people surely know that. Your car smells good right now, though."

"So what does he do? What's a date like for old people?"

"*Experienced* people, Damani."

"Right."

"There's no pressure. He makes his own wild-garlic pesto."

"I don't even know what that is."

"It's delicious. He sells produce at the market in town. That's where we met, you know. He's a gentleman. Garlic breath and all. He fought in the Vietnam War. Spends all his time on his allotment now. It's a lot bigger than what we got around by the community gardens. He walks dogs in the afternoon. Says it keeps his hips mobile and he feels twenty when he thrusts."

"He said that? The devil."

"He has gorgeous hands. Working hands. And his memory is impeccable. It would be nice to not use my timer so much. Good mobility, strong mind, all his own teeth. I think. Perfection, in any case."

"That's all it takes?"

"He's a parcel of goodness. He went on and on about confetti coriander. He's going to make videos all about the benefits of comfrey. I told him that's too niche. People want to be entertained these days. Comfrey may be fascinating, but it's no blockbuster plant."

"You don't think he was trying too hard?"

"No, no. He's just a dreamer. He even asked me if I'd co-host his new video collection."

"You're going to start vlogging?"

"He said my face was so pretty people would watch in flocks just to hear what I had to say. I said yes, because there really is no trouble in being happy. When you live, truly live, you let go. You try new things, and you learn about yourself. There's no making mistakes." Her cheeks warmed to a romantic maroon as deep as the reds in her beety brooch. Though Mrs. Patrice moved slowly, she moved spontaneously through life, with vigor and enviable confidence. I pulled up in front of her apartment and parked my car.

"All righty, Mrs. P., you big internet star." I turned and looked sincerely at her still-gorgeous eyes. The back window framed her bust and she may as well have been a painting. "I still got that vibrator if you need it, and some packs of gum for your stinky new stud."

She hit my arm with her hand. "Maybe I'll take the gum next time, Damani. You know, there's a pair of pregnant cats around here. Management will probably leave poison out for them after they sell the kittens."

"I got a water dish in the back and some cat food I can leave out."

"All in the trunk?"

"I have all sorts of things back there."

"Leave out the cat food, then. That would be nice. Come upstairs after, I'll make a pot of tea."

"Not today, Mrs. P. On the road is where the money's at. You know how it is."

"Fine. And when you're done, spray your car with more of that stuff. Whatever it is, it's working."

49

I left Mrs. Patrice's place and hoped for a ping. I drove around and around but something felt off. I moved my back while I sat on my seat and stretched my neck to either side while holding the steering wheel. Regardless, the feeling wouldn't go away.

Mrs. Patrice didn't live in the best neighborhood, but it wasn't so bad. A few blocks away, people had a harder time, a few blocks further and suddenly there were people who made six figures and slept most of the day.

In the park at the heart of the city that night, thousands gathered with tents, platforms, and megaphones. Signs and causes melded into a pastiche of demands, as a group of people wove through with the longest banner I'd ever seen, a thread that bound all the corners of the placards together: **Socialism will fix all of this.** As I drove, I scoped the perimeter of the open green space that the people of the city hung on to for air, sometimes to breathe, sometimes to stave off the inevitable. I read flashes of signs painted in black, neons, red, and white.

Black Lives for Palestine

The Fight for Climate Change Is the Fight Against Capitalism

Anti-Racism = The End of Exploitative Power

F*ck Heteronormativity

FUCK the Patriarchy

(In fact, there were plenty of FUCK-this signs.)

Dismantle White Supremacy

Boycott, Divest and Sanction CAPITALISM

Free Assange and All Political Prisoners!

ACAB!

The Police & Army CANNOT Protect Us Here or There

Working-Class People of the World Unite

BLACK TRANS LIVES MATTER!

Climate Justice Is Gender and Racial Justice!

Refugees Are People!

Somewhere in the crowd between a pair of weeping willow trees, I saw a stand set up by drivers.

Workers' Rights for ALL Workers!

Drivers Are Tired of Waiting

I knew Shereef was there in the crowd somewhere, Stephanie and Toni too. I squirmed in my seat, thinking that I could get out of my car and join them, but I needed at least three more pings to end the night and I was hoping for larger tips because the fare charges wouldn't be enough. I could've been there with the rest of the city, but I wasn't. Baa, baa. Who were the sheep anyways? I wanted to be one of those people holding megaphones, leading crowds into chants. I was useless in my car, even though I was essential and working in order to survive. I was nobody if I wasn't there.

I circled around the park again, thinking some folks would leave soon, but I wasn't getting a ping; maybe something was wrong with my connection. With my window down I stuck my phone out, hoping my signal would strengthen, but the bars didn't budge and anyway I already had four which was close to the maximum. On one side of the street, police officers formed a closed border. Some were bored, some embarrassed to be seen, and a few others rubbed their batons on their sides, feigning big-badge energy. Then there were the random pairs laughing with each other because they thought everyone with a placard was out of their mind. As I turned the bend, watching the spectacle of people through my wing mirror, I heard raised voices over the rolling of traffic, which was moving too slowly. Two officers held a woman, and two others beat a man to the ground with their batons, all of them becoming smaller as I drove away.

50

I leaned against the bar at Doo Wop, finishing up a ginger ale with the tiniest splash of brandy in it, playing with an ice cube in my mouth. I was still logged on to the app.

I kept thinking, What if I had driven back? What if I had honked my horn? What if I had stayed logged on, but with the demonstrators? I wanted Toni, Steph, and Shereef to keep vigilant, so I was reluctant to message them. I wondered if Jolene was at the park, and if she even knew what was happening to some folks out there.

"The police came by again. I'm telling you, something is in the air," said Alex from behind the bar as they wiped glasses with a damp cloth, looking up at a screen where Jimi Hendrix was playing his upside-down guitar with his teeth. My phone buzzed and I reached for it quickly. It was Amma. *There's no electricity!* I couldn't ignore it, so I wrote, *I left all the information out for you to make the payment. You didn't call the company?* Amma responded swiftly. *I was busy.* I started typing and then deleted the paragraphs I had written, knowing that bringing up how I practically learned to read just to take care of their paperwork and bills wasn't the right thing to do.

I took a sip from my glass, wishing Alex and I weren't so responsible and that there was more brandy in my drink.

"I think there's going to be an update sent out soon. Heard folks talking at the back. The cops have been waiting to raid us again," said Alex.

"Do they know about the . . ." I was hesitant to finish my sentence.

"Undocumented workers," they whispered, "and all the organizing . . . Hugo's already asking if he can hide his cigars somewhere. And Shereef was saying something about striking drivers camping out here. Not sure that'll be possible."

A beat of silence passed between us.

"I have to go," I said, spitting the last bit of ice I had in my mouth back in the glass.

"Already?"

"Yeah, my phone keeps buzzing. Ma has been alone for too long." I got up to leave and then remembered I had Anthony's business card in my pocket. "If Steph or Shereef stop by, give this to them for me. The guy loves assertiveness. Needs someone to crunch numbers. I don't know him, but he's rich and Steph has a math degree." I handed it to Alex and headed outside, hearing them shout, "I'll put it on the job board, I know three people with math degrees!"

51

Though it wasn't hot in my car, I felt sweaty. What if something else terrible happened? What if I didn't get any pings tomorrow? What if I couldn't pay all the bills? What if Jolene thought I was too eager or too closed off? Would I be a traitor if I moved in with her tomorrow? I knew I had to breathe but there was no air in my car. Undoing my seat belt, I stepped outside. Breathe in, four, three, two, one. Breathe out, one, two, three, four.

I grabbed my phone to message Jolene back. *I'm not sure about us,* I started, but then I quickly deleted that and wrote, *I'd like to see you soon too. D xxx*

52

It was eleven p.m. and destined to be one of those never-ending nights. I had to make up the hours I lost from our trip to the beach; there was no choice but to work late. I lifted heavy before I headed out again. I wanted to feel the ache of my muscles sooner rather than later, I wanted each last rep to end with my limbs shaking. Jolene said I looked like I was in shape and I didn't like that I was thinking this much about her and the things she said. I wanted to concentrate on something else. I knew I wouldn't get much sleep with my mind wired. My body ached from lifting and driving, and maybe from stress. Maybe it was all in my shoulders. I did stretch before driving and that always helped. I was about to do some Russian dead lifts and five sets of good mornings when Jolene messaged again: *I really can't stop thinking about you. Maybe we can go to my summer house next weekend? Or meet me for yoga? Whatever you want to do. Tell me where, tell me when, and I will cum.* Why did she spell it that way?

I knew I'd make her Pa's Deviled Beef sandwich at some point if we carried on together as whatever we could be. No one in Hot Kitchen knew it yet, but Appa taught me all I know about food. I made his sandwich as good as he did, because it was something that he put in the beef but hadn't included in the recipe. Something no one else in the kitchen had in the same way, even if they had it in their own way. I'd take Jo to Doo Wop for a two-dollar coffee that was made over an open flame. She'd save money and I'd kiss her when she realized how good our life could be together. What was I thinking? I couldn't help it. I knew our lives could be so good together.

53

"*It's just one of those things, isn't it? How we love to hate ourselves. The angsty teenager grows up to write the best music, doesn't she? The angry bird grows up to have the best sex. But enough of us glorifying our sadness. Self-harm is not cool! Let me show you something. And I want to stress, I appreciate how dedicated my followers are. I appreciate your trust. Don't mind Coco. Coco, you'll get your kibble later.* [The white cat meowed in the background, rubbing against Dr. H.'s leg.]

"*This is my stomach. Saggy, stretchy, stunning. Imagine I was sad. Punching myself would not give me the satisfaction I need to carry on. Ouff. See? Ouff. It's really not doing anything. Ouff. It serves no purpose. Ouff.*"

"Oh my God! Can you turn that off?" demanded the woman in my backseat who I assumed had fallen asleep.

"Huh? Yeah, sure. It helps me stay awake," I said, switching off Dr. Thelma Hermin Hesse, knowing that after this last passenger, I'd soon be in bed.

54

The next morning, somehow, I dropped off Mrs. Patrice, picked her up, and then came home for a short nap. On the other side of town, there's another Mademoiselle Ethiopia Café. There are actually a few in the city. Online it said that at this particular location, there was a patio, and from the reviews, it was twenty-five square meters smaller than the one Jolene visits, where she makes herself snug on the two-seater by the bay-view window. That afternoon, I had dropped off a passenger at a dental clinic in the unit opposite so I figured I would go in, unbeknownst to Jolene because people like me don't step into cafés like Mademoiselle Ethiopia, unless we're out with our generous girlfriends.

The waft of coffee and the café's brand blend of frankincense and grapefruit roused my senses and took me back to Jolene. The dark colors were brought to life with the natural light that came through the large windows, and the gold seats made the entire experience feel like opulence made affordable for some. Hanging from the ceiling, a chandelier spun ever so gently as it did in Jolene's favorite location, casting prisms of light that flashed in my eyes.

"Are you going to order?" Someone tutted behind me.

"Oh, right. Yeah." I was left with no choice, trapped in a labyrinth of a line with an overwhelming number of selections looming over me.

"What can I get you?" asked a barista whose name tag read *Paulina*.

"Your coffee is overpriced."

"Excuse me?"

"Can I have . . . that banana?"

"Sure. That's two-ten, please."

"Jesus. And the apple?"

For the record, because it's important that some things stay on record, I did not enter the café expecting to bump into Jolene. In fact, I was sure she wouldn't be here because it was past three on a Thursday and that was the day she held her after-school club. I did, however, want to feel her again like her cashmere blanket swaddling me.

I think I may have felt her before I heard her, because a current passed from the nape of my neck, pulsing over each of my discs. It trickled down and like a soft finger in a flower, it fluttered at my clit. In her smooth voice that I was learning could take my breath away, she said, "Damani?" So convincing in the way she pronounced the syllables of my name like only my mother does, *Tha-ma-nee*.

"What are you doing here?" I asked, surprised to see her.

"I had to follow up on a family around here. For work. I can't believe it!"

"You can be honest. Have you been following me, Jo?"

"Maybe."

"Come on," I said, smiling and rolling my eyes.

She snatched me out of the line and handed me her coffee cup so I could take a sip. Her blush-pink lip shade kissed the rim and on my lips, kissed me. "Would you be freaked out if I was following you?" Jolene smiled and all I was thinking was, Take me home, please.

"I'd be surprised, maybe. But no. You don't scare me," I said, expecting her to tease me with a witty response. Instead, she just pulled me towards a seat. Sitting across from me, she held my hands, and for a second I wondered if she was going to tell me we were a mismatched pair that couldn't thrive in the real world together. She brushed her nose and played with the dried stains left on the sides of the cup from trickling coffee.

"So, after I messaged you, I went for a run at the track by my house."

"It wasn't Sunday, though?"

She smiled, surprised that I remembered. "D., I'm actually quite unpredictable."

"I've noticed."

"And you haven't really seen how."

"You are here, unannounced."

"And so are you." She laughed, gazing into my eyes, and stroked the cup with her fingers. "Anyway, while I was running, this dog ran straight towards me and pounced. She was so strong I fell to the ground. Then, get this, she starts licking my face. And you know what? Are you ready for this?"

"I was born ready."

"Are you sure?"

"Are you kidding me? Look at me, Jolene."

This time she rolled her eyes, smiling, and carried on: "The dog looked just like my dog."

"The one who passed away?"

"Yeah. Just like Hadley." Jolene's eyes filled with tears and she tucked her lips inward. Her face flushed and her earlobes warmed to a crimson red. "I think it was her. That's possible, right? You believe in that, don't you?"

I wasn't sure what I believed about reincarnation. Empathy towards understanding towards change, right? So I thought, What would I do if a man, who looked just like Appa, pinned me to the ground and licked my face? I would knock the shit out of him. But seeing Jolene the way she was in front of me, I felt tender in my chest, engulfed by a warmth that rose inside of me. She needed a new therapist. A new pet? Someone to talk to and I could be that somebody. I couldn't tell if she was insulted, devastated, or in love with the spontaneity of life. People who have it all have problems, albeit interesting problems, too.

"That was probably really overwhelming. Maybe even beautiful," I said, unsure if I should hold her with an "I'm so sorry" or "Oh wow, what are the chances" hug. If she could open her whole summer house for me, if she could open up her heart to me, of course, I could open up my mind.

Jo dabbed her right tear duct and said, "And when it happened, you were the only one I wanted to tell."

55

"So what does she do? She live with her parents?" asked Stephanie, eyeing the houses that looked nothing like either of ours. We were parked on the curb outside Jolene's house and we might have been on a movie set. Every house in my view had clean gutters, fresh-cut grass, and flower beds that were in full bloom. On one lawn there was a sign that read *Bunnies Welcome* and there was a basket positioned in a corner full of carrots and shriveled leaves of lettuce.

"She's living the dream."

"Should I be nice to her or should I be normal?" Stephanie tapped her pumps on the mat when she asked.

"Be both."

She put on a coat of lipstick, looking at the mirror on the sun visor across the passenger side, puckering to finish. She didn't need another layer. The mauve she had on fit perfectly within the painted lines she had made. She tried my aviators on and studied her reflection with her mirror face, before putting them back on the dashboard. Stephanie was sexy and smart and not just anyone could mess with her. She looked at me leaning against the window, smiling.

"What?"

"Nothing." Steph grinned. "Toni got us a table."

"Nice."

"We'll have fun tonight. Shereef's been at Doo Wop for a few hours already."

"He's taking a break?"

"Says there's lots to do," she said.

I held the wheel tight, squeezing it until my fingers were numb, looking towards Jolene's house, wondering if she had changed her mind. I peeled a layer of skin from my lips, before putting some lip balm on. "I'm pretty sure Shereef's aunt used to live in this area. A lot of his family does, I think," Steph offered.

"On the other side," I said, because I knew the area well.

"Yeah, there used to be a really good shawarma place around here, right?"

"Closed down, for sure."

"There's that jerk chicken spot, though," Steph remembered.

"And a roti joint run by a guy named Kyle Cole."

"You got any spray?" she asked.

"The stuff that smells like pine and sex. It's in the glove box."

Stephanie popped it open and took out my switchblade. She played with it in her hands, looking fierce with her black nail polish. Shereef had a knife too, but mine was sharper. She handed it to me before taking out the bottle of cologne, which she sprayed on my wrists, neck, and chest. "Only you could pull off this smell." While we waited, she studied my face, examining my features for crust, whiteheads, or fallen brow hairs. "You look good," she said, brushing something off my nose before holding my hand. "You're sweating."

"Hardly."

"She makes you nervous?"

"A little."

"I've never seen you this way." She laughed. "You're wearing the ankle-strap heels I gave you."

"So?"

She placed her hand on my thigh. "With those little shorts and that tank, you know you look sexy, right?"

I flexed for her, laughing.

"Meow," she purred.

"You look good too," I threw back at her, smelling each of my underarms.

"I know," she teased, taking a sip of water while she looked out the window because Jolene's presence demanded her to. "Is that her?" Steph was judging and studying every bit of Jo as she walked towards my car. She was wearing a loose white T-shirt with a lacy bra underneath, tucked into a short red skirt.

"Is that velour?" I adjusted my seat, struggled with my belt, felt the scissors under the mat on my foot, and finally got myself out of the car, rushing to open the back door.

"Hey." Jolene blushed and touched my face with her cold hands. I noticed her rings and a silver bracelet that dangled off her wrist. She kissed me, holding on to my lips for longer than just any hello, and I was buried in a garden of periwinkles. She rubbed my lips with her thumb. "Lipstick," she said.

"This is Stephanie."

"Hi, Steph." Jolene's voice was warmer than usual. She touched Stephanie's shoulder as she stepped into my car, and felt comfortable enough to shorten Stephanie's name right away, to a single syllable. "This is for you, Damani." She handed me a bag before putting her seat belt on.

"Open it," said Steph, leaning against the dashboard, watching us approvingly as I got back in my seat. In the bag, wrapped in pastel-green tissues, was a card. I pulled it open, not knowing what to expect. If anything, I thought maybe it would play a song off of one of those thumb-sized speakers, which, interestingly, I knew cost as little as a dollar. But when I opened the card, half the earth popped out with two women sitting on top. *Together we can take on the world,* it read.

"My friend has a 3D printer," said Jolene.

"You know someone with a 3D printer?" I asked.

"People still own printers?" Stephanie chimed in. Jolene laughed.

"I know, right?" She smiled.

"I need a fucking printer," Stephanie mumbled to herself. I placed the card on my dashboard, smiling at Jolene in my rear-view thinking, Who really are you, Jolene?

56

The moon in the sky that night had been drawn with chalk and then smudged by someone's finger. Somehow the lights from Doo Wop reflected a halo above the space, making it look even more like heaven on earth, created for anyone with reasonable dreams. The bass of the music could be felt from outside, rumbling the ground, inviting us in.

"I didn't know this place existed," said Jolene as we walked through the blackberry bushes.

"People squat in a lot of the abandoned buildings around here," said Stephanie. The popping crack of fireworks set off in a bin banged like thunder in a barrel. Jolene jumped. I should've known then she was nervous, but of course I didn't think anything of it.

Let me slow down. Hugo was more agitated than normal, pacing near the entrance. Compared to the average Friday night, there were more people sitting around the picnic benches and hanging out by the tents while a stereo blasted something someone had recorded in a basement somewhere. You know when you can feel tension, or sense when people have just had sex? There was a cracking sense of something looming that was so tangible it made the hairs on my arms rise for a second. I noticed how people looked at Jolene.

"Got any—" I started, having stopped to speak to Hugo.

"No! I don't sell shit here," he snapped, biting his nails.

"He's usually a lot nicer," I said to Jolene, my hand on the small of her back.

Inside, Doo Wop was on another vibration. The D.J. was exceptional that night and though some people were sitting at tables huddled in deep discussion, many more were on the dance floor becoming spirits.

"Yes!" I exclaimed. Parts of my body were pulled by this force called Time Off, Logged Off, with music.

Stephanie laughed, connecting to the energy, and she danced with me as I raised my arms and shot my hips—left, right, left, and around to the beat. Jolene's eyes were on me. I was her personal little hip-swayer; the moment was all mine. I smiled at her.

"Here comes trouble!" welcomed Toni, walking towards us.

Jolene was quick. "I'm Jolene," she said, hugging Toni, rubbing her shoulders to seal the greeting. "I love your romper."

"This old thing. I got it for thirty bucks, so thanks for noticing," laughed Toni.

Jolene took in the space around her; her pupils grew large then small again, and the blues of her eyes caught the lights above. It was obvious how much she stood out against the browns of the walls, against the posters that were slapped on with tape, how she was a cutout over the paintings where most of us were camouflaged against each brushstroke. By the way she held herself it was clear that Jolene wasn't used to being a minority.

I had said to Jolene, practically shouting because the music was loud, "Let me get you a drink. Alcohol or no?"

"Alcohol, please." She looked at me, and I realized I was still standing in front of her. She smiled. "Did you want me to get it? Wait, take this at least." She took out a twenty from her purse.

"No, no. Okay, thanks. You have something in your hair." I pretended to pick out something from some strands just under her cheek and she placed the money in my hand. I walked towards Stephanie and Toni, who were at the bar, and I was surprised Jolene didn't follow me. I took it as a good sign.

"So, she's cute," said Toni. "She's still for tomorrow or are you playing the field?"

"That's not cool these days, is it?"

"Not unless you both want that."

"Going to her summer house next week."

"Summer house, eh."

Alex leaned against the bar, taking Steph and Toni's orders.

"Brandy and lemon?" Alex asked me.

"Two tonight," I said.

"Oh, okay." Alex made a face; they were surprised but pleased that I was making new friends.

We raised our glasses and took a sip of our chosen poisons. I held Jolene's glass and waited for Steph and Toni to walk away as I watched her from the bar. Jolene in action was a gazelle in the vast wilderness, hiding behind a shrub, peeking between branches, waiting for the right time to simply be. Shereef was sitting with others, drivers I was sure. He was rocking a pair of dark jeans and a patched denim shirt that I wanted to borrow. Steph started rolling a blunt, the christening to the end of the week, though I'd work that weekend, as I did on most. She licked the tobacco wrap and pinched and pulled it tight. I didn't want to be too far from Jolene's side—I felt I needed to protect her, but I was protective of my people too. The D.J. spun a mix of hip-hop tracks from underground to indie to nineties classics. Then he put on some Snoop Dogg, and Jolene nodded approvingly before making her way to the dance floor alone.

Everyone saw her, but everyone carried on as if she wasn't there. Then, it was Shaggy. It must've been someone like Shaggy. Jolene put her hands in the air, letting go, revealing she was made of feathers. She wanted me to notice just how light she was. I took another sip of my drink and I would've been just fine watching her from the sticky bar, but I had her drink and maybe she was thirsty. I danced my way back over, unbothered by the eyes on her. I was her luvvah, luvvah, and she called me funtastic.

"The music!"

"Yeah, it's great here." I handed over her drink. "My dad used to come home after working a long day. Which was pretty much every day. He'd have a glass of brandy with a whole lemon squeezed into it."

"A whole lemon?"

"A whole lemon. If you don't make a face, there's not enough."

She took a sniff, then a sip, looking into my eyes. Her red lipstick, faintly smudged on the rim. The expression on her face revealed it was just right. She blew from her pursed mouth, blowing fire into my face.

"You like?"

"It's strong."

"Then it's perfect."

"Cheers." She pressed her lips against the glass before she took another sip, moving her shoulders to the rhythm. Her body was close to mine and it was obvious that we both wanted to be near each other. We clinked glasses. The track switched into a magical mix of James Brown and Biggie Smalls. I couldn't sustain a conversation with her while it played. She moved closer to me with brandy on her lips, her chest so close to mine that if the music stopped, she'd feel my heartbeat.

"Dance with me," I said, even though she had already taken the lead. Jolene held my hand and found her way against my hips. I turned her, so we were face-to-face again. We were so warm together, I wanted to take my clothes off. Her fingers followed the curves of my body, and I wanted her to bite into my skin. I pulled her even closer, feeling her breasts on my chest. I kissed her neck and felt her legs open and close, gripping onto mine. The music stopped but only for a second and we laughed, realizing there were people all around us. She took a deep breath and sipped her drink.

"You okay?" I asked. She pulled me close but not too close. I went in for a kiss but she stopped; looking at my lips, she smiled. "That was fun." Steph was heading towards us with the blunt in her mouth as Toni walked beside her, occasionally busting out a groove. I pushed Jolene playfully, then pulled her closer again. Seeing the four of us, Shereef made his way over too. Stephanie smiled as we huddled close on the dance floor in communion, and Toni pulled out her lighter from her bra, lighting the tip of the blunt we had waited all week for. Jolene's nostrils flared from the earthy smell.

"We're inside," she said.

"You don't have to if you don't want to," I said, noticing a formation of sweat on the tip of her nose.

"It's cool," she said, looking around. "Do the police come here?"

"Why would they come here?" asked Steph suspiciously.

"It's cool," I said to her. "They don't," I said to Jolene. Steph passed me our version of the Eucharist—the tobacco paper the bread, the cannabis the blood—and I took a puff, a puff, and another puff to the perfect amount of mellow.

"If they ever did . . ." Steph started, exhaling perfect circles from her lips.

"Honestly, we're this close to bombing the RideShare headquarters, they'd better not," laughed Shereef. And come on, we all knew he was joking. He had only come over to hold Stephanie as we smoked all our troubles away. I passed the blunt to Jolene and made sure with my eyes she was okay with it. Hesitant, she nodded and took a tiny, sweet draw. Then she took another, her blue eyes scanning the entire space again. As we laughed and spoke over each other, she held my hand, every so often looking the other way. I held her face and kissed her cheek.

"You okay?"

"Yeah. I'm good," she said, and I believed her.

57

The ice in my glass was melting from the heat of the bodies all around, and from my breath each time I placed the glass to my mouth. I sucked a few cubes and spat them back in my drink, shooting them slowly into my glass so no one noticed. Condensation dripped down the sides, my lips were wet. Four of us sat at a table. Toni had gone to the restroom. In the center was our little fire pit in the form of a red waxed candle made by an addiction support group. It flickered in front of us, casting shadows on our faces. Jolene had her legs crossed with one hand on the table and the other on my lap, gripping my knee as if worried that if she didn't hang on tight, she'd slip and fall through the floorboards unnoticed.

Shereef's hands were clasped on his closed notebook. He took a gulp of water then wiped his mouth with the back of his hand. Leaning in close to me he whispered, "I'm happy you're trying." His breath fresh like spearmint, mine like burned cigarettes.

"Is he into you?" whispered Jolene, smiling while looking at Shereef, before looking at me and back at Shereef again.

"What? He's a brother."

"Of course. I'm only kidding," she said, tapping her fingers on the old palette tabletop, each finger a solid note. I did worry she was tripping; blunts are stronger than spliffs, and she wasn't used to it.

"Damani, I didn't fill you in. What's about to unfold . . . I can feel it in my bones. Things are going to finally topple over," said Shereef, beaming, the lights around him warming his complexion.

"It's a pretty outrageous plan. I love it, at least," said Steph, rubbing Shereef's back.

"I'm looking forward to hearing about it." And I said that because even though we were in a safe place, some things mustn't be discussed so loud.

"What's the plan?" Jolene interjected. In a second, she had effortlessly stripped off the skin of a gazelle with perked ears, listening for footsteps over fallen leaves, and become a hunter with a loaded gun, eyeing every corner. Stephanie still had the blunt in her hand. She could smoke until she reached a hairline of the filter, she wasn't one to waste. A cloud blew in our faces as her eyes moved to each side. Shereef thumbed the coil binding of his notebook in front of him, watching Steph, watching us. His eyes were unsure when they met mine. He cracked his knuckles and the clicks ran a shiver up my spine. Jolene didn't know where to look. Her eyes darted from our candle fire pit, the sandy hues of our table, Shereef's notebook and water, the level of alcohol in each of our glasses, the ashtray, a cemetery for tobacco and wild herbs. Her fingers still scratched into my knee. It wasn't until after I'd looked into her cobalt-blue eyes for ten innocuous seconds that she dared look towards Shereef and Stephanie again. The showdown started with our glances before they turned to full stares. Shereef licked his lips, then swallowed. One thick hair from his nostril reached the top of his moustache. Steph's eyeliner was a perfect black streak. She finally outed the roach in the ashtray, twisting the butt to dust. The whites of her eyes were red with cracks, as I knew mine were. She got out eye drops from her purse and offered the bottle to me. I shook my head, no. Leaning her head back, she squirted a few drops into each of her eyes. I looked at her and blew her a kiss. Jolene saw. She looked down before looking my way. Then she rubbed my knee over the imprints of her nails.

"It's for drivers and riders." Shereef took a sip of his water.

"Oh my God! Stop! I could plan a demonstration. I've been to plenty in the past few days alone. I can organize the permits." Jolene was revitalized and I was happy she was comfortable. She loosened her grip on my knee, and now both of her hands were on the table. No guns, no weapons, no malice; innocent until proven guilty.

"That's great. But that's not what we need right now, you know?" Shereef said.

I looked at Stephanie, knowing her eyes were on me. We both looked straight at Jolene.

"But everyone is out on the streets. It could really add to the momentum. Since the Women's March I—"

"Drivers and riders have organized marches. It's not new. *We* are out there already."

"No, of course! Absolutely. We have to honor all those who marched before us, for sure." Jolene ran a hand through her hair, twisting the ends. She added, "But I have access—" Stephanie and I looked at each other again, both hoping the next clause of Jolene's sentence would be redeemable. "I have access to a great café and we've taken action there already. Raising funds, spreading awareness."

"That's fantastic. Everyone has a role to play."

"Absolutely. And there's so much work to be done. I'd be really honored to help."

"I'm really appreciative of that but I think we're okay. These days fundraising and spreading awareness isn't cutting it."

"Of course, and we can do more. We have to. But I will say, my group can make a big difference."

"Making yourselves feel good doesn't count," mumbled Steph.

"Hey, come on," I pleaded through gritted teeth— *please, no one ignite this shit.*

"It's okay, D. I want to do this without it being about me. My team for the most part are doing the work, and then some, while spotlighting grassroots activists like yourselves."

"I'm sure you are, and that's great," said Shereef. "But we have our plan under control. Thanks for offering to help, though."

Up until this showdown, I had only seen about fourteen expressions from the plethora of Jolene's possible faces. The Jolene who sat beside me leaned forward; her top lip quivered and not because my mouth was to her ear.

"You're not really going to bomb a building, are you?" she asked.

"Excuse me?"

"Let's dance!" I said, hoping to keep the promise of our future. My bags were practically packed and I was ready for life at the summer house, rhubarb crumble, and Prosecco every Friday.

"I'm just saying, violence isn't the answer."

"You asked me a very loaded question," Shereef fired back.

"I'm sorry you felt it was loaded. But you said earlier—"

"I'm not going to sit here and talk about violence, who gets to use it and who gets punished for it."

"Oppression is violence in itself," added Steph, to which I nodded an amen. Of course I agreed with her, but Jolene looked at me with an "Are they serious?" drop of her jaw.

"I hear you and I'm listening. I just think that it's important we all get involved in issues without the aggression," said Jolene, switching her gaze back on Shereef and Steph.

"Who's being aggressive?" asked Steph. Jolene's eyes scanned across all of our faces. We stared back.

Enunciating, she said, "I just feel like things are getting unnecessarily heated."

"I think you've misunderstood something," said Shereef.

"What I'm trying to say is that I'd really like to help drivers and riders too. My girlfriend is a driver, after all," blurted Jolene, and she hadn't even had her second drink. Stephanie looked at me with her mouth open. Girlfriend? I had a girlfriend before I even knew it myself. "My girlfriend is Brown. I mean, of course I get it."

"Brown? Are you kidding me?" said Steph.

"Did I say something?"

"You think by association you somehow get it? I thought you'd know better."

"Steph, just leave it," said Shereef.

"No, I'm serious."

"Of course not, Stephanie. I have a lot to learn, but I am aware that things are different for me compared to Damani. And I'm doing the work."

"Fucking hell. I can't do this."

"Why are you getting so angry?" asked Jolene.

"This is not me angry, sweetheart," said Steph.

"Then I'm sorry you're upset. Maybe it's best to reconvene when we're all calm, then. This doesn't need to be so intense."

"All right, Jolene. Basically—" Shereef's dark, majestic eyes looked at his lover's and then at mine and I knew it in my heart, but I couldn't accept it. Jolene and I had connected and clearly she was imperfect but I could teach her, I could change her! It wasn't over, though. Shereef was a careful man, a chess player with his actions and words. But I was worried about what he was going to say.

One wrong inflection could crush Jolene into pieces that I wouldn't know how to put back together. He leaned forward on the table and I prayed he wouldn't say something I couldn't fix. His eyes stared into Jolene's. She leaned closer. "If we went on strike—" he started.

"I could help raise awareness for the strike," Jolene said, almost yelling, her hands clasped on her heart.

"If we went on strike, our demands are—"

"For more money?"

Shereef stared at her. "If we went on strike, our demands are for ownership, as in all these rich folks step down, and we flip their scheme into a cooperative. That way we all have equal say in matters because we're the ones affected by decisions made at the top. We should be making those decisions. But the company, or more accurately the shareholders, don't want that."

"Hmm. Maybe we could offer social justice training to the people qualified to manage, though."

"Sorry?"

"So yes, we can strike but we'll get more publicity if you change your demands. There are drivers who want driving to be just a gig thing, you know. It's not their 'job' and working for a big company works for them."

"There's a huge disparity between what drivers make and what the shareholders make. Plus, who says a driver doesn't have the ability to manage themselves?" Jolene made a noise in the back of her throat and everyone's eyes slid over to her. She was raising her eyebrows and looking down at the table. "Is there something—" Shereef started.

"It feels like you're patronizing me."

"I apologize, Jolene," said Shereef.

Jolene sighed, taking a moment for herself. Then she said, "The system is evil. It's grinding people down, I get it, but we can make it work. Change the company's vision. Make the drivers employees, give them benefits, incentives. That's all plenty of drivers want. I read about it online. Drivers can be board members if they want to. They can even buy shares. I saw RideShare already gives money to charities too."

"Jolene—" Shereef said, his eyes closed, his right hand stroking his chin. Steph and I watched, sat on the edge of our seats.

"We can help RideShare become a good example. They have the most diverse workforce out there. There are opportunities here."

"Listen, it's great you're excited about this. But we have a plan of action already that involves a group of us working together."

"So, what is it?"

"I'm really tired and I don't think now is the time to go over things."

Jolene shook her head.

"Are you okay?" I asked.

"I'm just so tired of dealing with this in activist spaces. It's exhausting." My eyes have never found Stephanie's so quickly. Toni walked over, rubbing her hands with lotion.

"There's way too much water mixed into that hand soap," she said, taking a seat.

Looking at Shereef, Jolene continued. "You may not have noticed this, and I understand that you have a lot on your mind, but you've interrupted me about five times in this conversation. You even interrupted Damani and Steph. We have ideas too. Community organizing isn't a one-*man* show."

"Oh shit," someone whispered from the table beside us.

"Just because we're women doesn't mean we can't understand politics or organize. We have a lot to offer. I'm actually a social worker and have experience working with vulnerable people," Jolene continued. "Steph, you're a strong and fierce woman, you get what I'm saying, right?"

"Wow." Stephanie didn't hide a single emotion in her stare. "Tell me, when did Shereef interrupt me?"

"When you said that—"

"If Shereef interrupts me, that's for me to deal with. Not you. He interrupted *you* because *you've* gone on about some dangerous shit."

"Dangerous?"

"For one thing, we aren't 'vulnerable.' We're robbed of the money we're owed." Stephanie took a sip of her drink. She rubbed the top of her head, pushing down the loose hairs that frayed from her ponytail.

"Hmm, I'll bear that in mind moving forward. But there's no need to get so defensive. I don't know why everyone's attacking me now," said Jolene.

"So, I missed a lot?" Toni leaned in closer, looking for answers.

"She's just reasserting that she'd like to help with the cause," informed Shereef, his hands on his notebook, his body made small, his leg bouncing under the table.

"I wasn't trying to victimize anyone," said Jolene.

"I understand that," Shereef reassured.

"I really don't appreciate this aggression towards me. I'm just trying to help."

"I didn't mean to upset you, Jolene. I think we have different ideas for change, that's all," added Shereef.

"Because you're perfectly fine with the use of violence."

"You're going to take it there again?" asked Steph.

"Yes, I am, because I don't want to see another activist go down the wrong path."

Shereef wiped the sweat from his forehead. He leaned forward to speak, but stopped himself before trying again. "Just to be clear, Jolene," he began, his voice cracking. "There's nothing to worry about," reassured Shereef.

"But you did say something earlier."

In perfect synchrony, someone popped a bottle and they might as well have accidentally fired a gun. Pop! We all looked around, except for Jolene. Her eyes didn't leave Shereef's face.

"I don't remember what I said."

"I don't believe in violence, Shereef, and I'm not sure I believe you. Silence is violence and there's too much of that already." This time, Stephanie rolled her eyes and Shereef half-smiled. "Why are you laughing at me? I've read books on this."

"Written by whom?" questioned Toni, who by now had

gathered enough of the conversation to pick the right side.

"By lots of different people." Jolene studied all of our faces. The candle flickered and a strawberry scent passed through in the silence at our table. Jolene leaned back, shaking her head to herself. I imagined her inner monologue was raging, but what was she actually thinking? She opened her mouth to speak, then stopped herself. She leaned closer, licked her lips, and closed her eyes. "I'm not a racist," she said.

"Hey, hey, hey," I started.

A second "Oh shit!" came from the table beside us.

"No one said you were," said Toni.

Jolene shook her head, her face redder with the reflection of the candle burning in front of her. I got out a cigarette, lit it, and placed the pack on the table.

"Let's dance, guys. Let's not get into this tonight. Shereef had his five-years-of-sobriety a few days ago, and it's Friday night. Come on! Let's go."

"I have to get back to some work, but it was lovely meeting you, Jolene," said Shereef. He looked at me. "We can celebrate later."

"Nice to meet you too," she said as her hand found my lap again and her nails dug into my knee. "Could you believe that?" she whispered to me softly.

58

Dr. Thelma Hermin Hesse once threw out, in a video, something Mark Twain had said about how we can only know love after a quarter of a century. Dr. H. was on the hunt for a crush she had had twenty-five years ago, hoping there was a forest of love waiting for the both of them. My generation grew up differently, though. We knew love in brief moments: single smiles with a passing stranger on the train, in an exchange of awkward compliments via messages, in consistent likes received on our social media. In our minds we rolled through glades of bluebells in a euphoric awakening from our heavy lives whenever we felt an inkling of attraction and acceptance. As quick as we felt, we acted. We moved on impulse before we changed our minds and of course this was thrilling, but also the worst of all habits. What can we truly know if time hasn't shaped it? At least, that's been my experience. I took my time with Jolene, I thought. I was careful, worried she would bite my fingers off. Do not feed animals you do not know by name. Unless they're starving on the street and you can see pain in their eyes, their ribs exposed on their sides.

We were still seated at the table. Steph left to get drinks for us at the bar, and Toni was speaking to a friend nearby. Jolene hadn't said a word since they all departed. "Are you okay?" I asked her. Her voice shook and a blue vein made an appearance, pulsing from under her skin as if her forehead was a stage, her hair the curtains.

"That was not okay." The D.J. played another Shaggy track and I suddenly believed in a higher power again.

"Come here." I held her close to me.

"No, I'm serious, D.! Do you know something that I don't?"

"What?"

"I get that he's your friend, your brother or whatever, but . . . do you remember what happened after the two hundred refugees went missing? Someone set a bank on fire. That guy is up to something."

"I don't understand."

"You're too close to see it. He could be putting you all in a lot of danger, including himself."

"I think you need to chill maybe. Steph's getting another round. Let's enjoy the night?"

"Steph was also really rude to me."

"That's just how she talks."

"That's not an excuse. I'm fuming. I need to think."

"Think about what?"

"I know what I heard, Damani. I know what he said."

"Babe, maybe you're being a little bit paranoid? It happens to me too sometimes."

"Everyone is staring at me." Jolene's eyes were back on Shereef, standing in a group across from us. Most of them were drivers.

"Forget about him."

"You don't get it."

"Are you going to cry?"

"No!"

"Because you can cry."

"I have experience with violence and I don't want to see any more of it."

"Hey. No one has been violent," I said, caressing her face.

"Doesn't mean no one is going to be," said Steph, walking up to us. She placed a tray of drinks on the table, then punched my biceps.

I laughed, rubbing my arm even though she'd barely dented it.

"I got you a different drink, Jolene. I know Appa's concoction is a punch in the mouth."

"Thanks. I have to go to the bathroom." Jolene stood up. I reached for her arm, stood up with her, and kissed her cheek. I did not feel her face melt on my lips as it usually did. I smiled at her. "Why are you looking at me like that?" she asked.

"I want you to be happy. Take all the time you need, okay," I said, but Jolene had already walked the other way.

"So, that was intense," said Toni, sliding up to us.

"Honestly, I thought she was going to throw something. You know I don't get involved in certain discussions with certain people, but I couldn't just say nothing," said Steph.

"Should I be worried?" I asked.

"Let her cool off. She'll be fine. You'll figure it out," said Toni.

"Yeah, but Shereef."

"That man has the patience of a saint. He's got bigger fish to fry."

"But do me a favor, D. Just keep an eye on her," said Steph.

The three of us laughed about it for a while, shaking off the tension. My right foot had pins and needles suddenly, and the jitter pulled a cramp in my calf. We continued drinking, smoking, and dancing, one song, two songs, three songs, four, all the while I was thinking about Jolene. She wasn't at the bar and she wasn't on the dance floor. She wasn't in the bathrooms where she'd said she'd be. She wasn't having an intense conversation with anyone, sharing the story of our first kiss. She wasn't in the kitchen watching the chefs cook up a storm. She wasn't in the basement unfolding mats. She wasn't by the tents meeting interesting people, and Hugo wouldn't give me any information about who he saw. I ran outside to the back and the music faded behind me. Far from where people congregated in fellowship with mocktails, cocktails, shisha, beer, home-style food, and pitchers of water to wash it all down, I saw her pacing near the parking lot with her phone to her ear. When I walked over, she saw me.

I heard her heart drop and fall into her stomach with a sizzle.

59

"What's wrong?"

"I don't know. I—"

"Are you okay?"

"I overheard people talking outside."

"And?"

"That guy, Sheriff."

"Shereef. What about him?"

"He was with this group."

"Drivers."

"They had big sweaters."

"It's chilly."

"They were smoking."

"Cigarettes, most probably."

"I don't trust him. Five years of sobriety?"

"Yeah, it's incredible."

"He has a beard."

"So do I sometimes," I said, showing off my chin.

"They were loading a car. And shouting. People kept staring at me."

"Because you look different."

"I look normal, D.!"

"Listen, Jo."

"This place is unsafe. The ceiling is going to fall, the floors are unstable. The restroom is a mess. People were smoking cigarettes in the kitchen. I think there are sex workers in those tents. There were so many homeless people asking me for money."

"Wait, that's what you see here?"

Jolene sighed. "Sheriff and—"

"Shereef."

"He and these people were speaking, but I couldn't understand what they were saying. He doesn't seem like a nice guy, Damani. He's going to do something terrible."

"What . . . ? Jolene."

"What!"

I took a deep breath and clenched my lips tight before I asked, ". . . Who did you call?"

"I've seen this in people I've worked with. I'm sure he's had a difficult life and it's probably made him unstable. He's angry, Damani, I get that, we're all angry! But he's planning something. He *wants* to be violent." She looked around again showing me an article she found on her phone. "I've heard about this place, too," she said. "This place is a front, D. It's not safe and you don't belong here."

"*Who* did you call, Jolene?"

"I think we should leave. Kat's coming to get us."

"To get us?"

"I don't know if she'll find the place so we should go. Right now! Leave with me, D. We need to go now."

60

In another video once posted by Dr. Thelma Hermin Hesse, she said, "You've got to put your feet in someone else's shoes," and now she's selling used shoes for $33.50. "Look at these old size-ten basketball trainers I've been wearing. I now know what it feels to be undervalued, misunderstood, poor," she had said while the camera captured a close-up of the left shoe, the sole hanging off like a yapping mouth. I tried to imagine myself in Jolene's Oxfords, envisioning what it was she may have felt, what it was she may have seen at Doo Wop. She'd have come across faces that were unfamiliar to her. Smells that she didn't understand. Dark bodies lurking behind her, their shadows growing in size. People had danced their spirits free, hollering and laughing in the joys of the coming weekend, their feet stomping rhythms that warmed the ground. The English that Jolene had heard was sharpened with each of our own unique accents and slang, words broken and chopped into a song of a sentence. Our soup of words brewed in a pot shaped by history. Shakespeare would have written a sonnet inspired by our dissident use of language. Fourteen lines? Iambic pentameter?

Probably not. He knew too well how to break the rules. Sonnet 155:

Kadhal, love, born from a fear of letting go
Roja, rose, the color of her lips.
The yearning heart trembles at the thought of
  tomorrow
Where lovers slide and whine from chest to hips
Big up the folk dem massive!

As Jolene stood within our circle the multitude of clattering tongues in her ears must have taken her to a foreign place, far from anywhere she'd been to in the city. The horror. She might have walked around in search of familiarity, a pocket of comfort where she could rest, but there had been that aunty chatting about dismantling the entire makeup of the city with a hammer, a sickle and some paint—that must have really disoriented Jolene. She would've been still hanging on to the wounds from the word-slinging showdown. Maybe she realized that she could do more, that she had not done enough, that she was complicit in something bigger than herself, but everything she had ever been told said, "No, don't believe it!"

She would've run downstairs, stumbled about lost in a cave of supplies for those in need, fallen on the pile of mats. Following the music and the stomping, she'd have found her way back upstairs and around past the dance floor; she'd have gone outside where on an orange

L-shaped bench people chatted about life after capitalism, life with communism, and classlessness, and that just may have been it! The ugly C words may have triggered a chord in her spirit and she lost all means of rational thinking. Had she thought that Black lives mattered until her back was against the wall? Did someone whisper "racist" as she passed by, shooting the word off their tongue like a dirty dart dipped in poison? I tried to hear her voice in my mind, but it hurt my head to think about what she may have felt.

Damn it! I couldn't think! I needed a second to hang on to the future I imagined: Jolene and me. But as I had tried to inch closer, she had only tugged away. I took a deep breath in and then out again. I thought it might have been too dark inside for Jolene to properly see, and so she couldn't see outside either. Her vision may have blurred, it was normal to feel anxious. Anxiety attacks were as common as yawning these days. They just happened.

Or Jolene, shaken out of her conversion to allyship, backslid into what she knew best. She didn't think twice about it—it was too easy, almost natural. She knew exactly what she was doing and she actually thought I'd be okay with it. I was the exception. I was her validation.

61

Sirens blared in the distance, cutting through the cacophony around me. Inside my body there was a pounding, the butterflies from my stomach fluttered up and out through my mouth, half-burned in bile, quarter-tangled in slobs of spit. Jolene was a flower withering before my eyes. She was courageous, bold, and ugly.

"Come with me," she said. I wished I'd taken some time to find the answers in her stare. How? Why? I just didn't get it and there was no time to figure it out. I ran back into what she saw as the darkness. "Damani!" I had a responsibility to everyone inside.

"They're coming," I said to the waitstaff who I knew lived in the city without any legal documents. They ran inside to tell the others. "They're coming," I said to a woman I knew sold her sex in a tent outside. "Fuck! They're coming," I screamed to Shereef who had a knife in his pocket as I had, as all the drivers had too. He ran to tell others who were on probation, who had a crumb of cannabis lining their pockets, who had had previous encounters with the law. Those who had to, ran far and fast. Those who had nowhere to go ran straight to the D.J. booth, lifting up yellowing floorboards to get down into a hidden storage room. Those who could be found and questioned remained dancing because they still could, and they knew from the bottoms of their hearts that they were doing nothing wrong, and they might just protect someone else if they stayed.

I ran, having not seen Toni or Steph. Gripping the walls I stumbled outside. With the keys in the ignition I knew I had to go, but there was nowhere to be, except on an empty road that rolled and rolled out and into nowhere.

For the hours I was on my own with my high beams on, I gripped the wheel, worried my heart would explode. Someone would find me with my blood splattered on the windows. CLEAN ME, I'd have written, with my index finger sifting through the red clumps of me.

62

There was duct tape on the front door where there had been a chip near the lock because someone once tried to break in. Whoever the fuck wanted to break into our basement must've really been in need. A couple years ago, I'd chased three young men out of the house share I lived in. I ran outside with a butter knife, screaming, "Don't ever come back or I swear to your God that I will chop your body to pieces." They never came back. In fact, the next morning there was a single rose on the doormat taken from our neighbor's rosebush. I could tell because they were exactly the same, yellow with dark brown spots that slightly bled into Gaussian blurs. I thought of that butter knife when I opened the front door, maybe to remind myself that I am a badass bitch when I need to be.

I called Shereef's phone and Stephanie's. There was no answer. I called Toni and she messaged back: *On my way home, S Club was taken in for questioning.* Downstairs the television was loud and I worried that Amma was also losing her hearing.

"It was a good night for us and we're asking the public to remain alert. There are still a number of persons out there

at large who are engaging in antisocial behavior. They must be held to account."

"That was Superintendent Barlow at a press conference, after local law enforcement arrested eight illegal migrants for working without documentation. A twenty-five-year-old man and a forty-year-old man were also arrested for breaching their court bail, and an unusual quantity of knives and other bladed weapons have been confiscated after being found in a kitchen pot. 'The Doo Wop' has been rumored to have been on police radar for several years, and Superintendent Barlow believes it is a hotbed of drug trafficking, radicalization, and domestic terrorism. We'll tune back in now."

"We seized an amount of cannabis, and we have the dogs out now searching for more. We're dealing with a very organized group of dangerous radicals here and we know that people don't want to speak out of fear. We need the community's help. Any information we can get will be crucial at this point. We want to thank our informants in the neighborhood who were willing to stand up and share information with us. To quote one of our anonymous callers, being silent is being violent. Our job is to serve and protect our city. Locking up criminals, including illegal migrants and dangerous radicals, and keeping our streets safe, is what the public expects from us, and our officers are going to continue delivering that for the community. Yeah . . . uh, the floor is open for questions. Go ahead."

"Can you share more details about the investigation? How much cannabis was found?"

"*We have thus far seized a quantity of cannabis that we suspect is inconsistent with personal use. A sensitive terrorism investigation is also ongoing, and we will keep the media apprised of our progress.*"

The hallway appeared to be extending and the next thing I knew I was in the kitchen with a glass cup in my hand. There was a rustling coming from the living room and without a thought I smashed the cup on the counter, forgetting to let go. Shards pierced my palm, clinging to my skin. Blood dripped to the ground. One drop turned to a splatter at my feet and below me was art made from my body. Amma stuck her head out from the hallway; her eyes moved down to my chest as the television murmured behind her. Do mothers see broken hearts over clothes and skin and flesh? She looked at my hand, then down to the blood that had dripped onto my pants.

"Ah, Damani. Again?"

The only voice I could tune into over an annoying buzz that rang in my eardrums was Dr. Thelma Hermin Hesse's, playing in my head. "*Breathe in and out and count to four. Slowly this time.*" She had said in one episode that we need to deal with our emotions before they start having serious consequences in our lives. She hadn't yet mentioned what we ought to do when our whole life was an emotional vortex with the addition of knowing very well what is stacked against us at every corner. "What you ought to do, my dear followers, is write letters, deep and meaningful letters, then burn them in a bowl." I wondered if this was how Appa felt when his heart stopped.

63

The wrong thing to do would've been to remain lying in bed for longer than I needed to. It would feel a lot better to fall into this pit that was calling me to unravel into deep depths that would consume every bit of me. I couldn't afford to do that, though. My hand hurt, but my back hurt more from driving. My wrists ached. There was that tangle that wound the ligaments in my leg together with some other muscles I didn't know I had.

Something was burning. Amma was on the couch, hiding under her fleece cover. The television was on again and darkened bread popped out of the toaster. Two fried eggs were served on a plate for eyes, two slices of cucumber were ears, and a slice of tomato smiled upwards.

"Did you eat?"

"Don't worry about me today," said Amma.

I wanted to cheer her on and tell her how proud I was of her for getting up and attempting breakfast. That was more than she'd done in half a year, but I didn't have the time. Plus I woke up with the weight of carrying sandbags on my wrists. Maybe I resented her a little too. The bread was nearly burned, crisp but still edible. I almost choked. As I was about to leave with the faint scent of charred toast behind me, I knew very well I was doing something wrong, so I went back downstairs, kicked my high-tops off and walked towards Amma. Lifting the covers I said, "Thank you."

"Stay out of trouble, D. You know what people are like." Just before I left she added, "I love you, Damani. Don't ever forget, your Appa does too."

64

That morning Mrs. Patrice smelled of curdled milk and tea. I had called Jolene twenty-eight times already and heard nothing from Steph or Shereef. I wished I'd followed Jolene to the bathroom. I should have never let her out of my sight.

"I told my son, it's fine if you don't want to settle down again, but think about the children. Do you really want them to live between two houses?"

"I would've loved that."

"But he doesn't want to actually be anywhere. He wants to travel. He wants to—"

"Hey, Mrs. P., are summer houses gated?"

"I'm not sure. Depends. My son couldn't afford a summer house if that's what you mean."

Was a summer house a cottage made with logs or a house made light and airy? Probably nautical themed, probably with a big veranda or a conservatory with lounge chairs or something. For sure there was a cabinet with loads of alcohol, a tree swing made of sisal rope with an old tire for a seat, right?

"Why do you have Band-Aids on your hand? Was it the foxes again?"

"The what? Oh, yeah. The foxes. I think it's safe to say, I taste delicious."

"You need to inform your doctor, if you're blacking out again. It could be a wolf next time you're on the floor unconscious."

The goddesses will forgive me for lying to Mrs. Patrice. I once had a black eye and drying scabs with plasma oozing from cuts on my hand. I had told Mrs. P. that I had passed out in the woods and fallen victim to the hunger of foxes in heat. What had actually happened was, this woman took a hundred dollars from under my mattress after I licked her straight into bliss. With no shame, she couldn't care less that Amma was in the living room; she had wailed like a pig. While I was in the bathroom washing my mouth, she thought she could get away with her little pilfer, but I walked into the room having changed my mind about pissing. She called *me* a crazy bitch with *my* hard-earned cash in *her* hands. The entire room softened and then sharpened in focus, and I was suddenly outside of my body, looking down at myself. With the urge to punch her, I froze from having stared at her face for too long. I couldn't bring myself to lift my knuckles to her cheek, so I slapped her instead.

I wasn't proud of it, but violence *is* sometimes the answer. She was furious and I was pumped with adrenaline, so I told her to hit me back.

"Punch me," I had said. Without even thinking about it, she reached her arm back and punched my brow. "Again." The second punch was to the mouth and a harder blow.

Blood pooled from between my teeth and I spat in her face because we were both pieces of shit and nothing felt good about that. The woman, whose cum was down my throat by then, smashed a glass, picked up the pieces, and held my hand so the shards pierced our palms together. Fucking psycho, right?

Dr. Thelma Hermin Hesse did an episode on what she called disassociation. It was possible to disconnect from the world around us. She had said, "Sometimes we do horrible things because we weren't breastfed for long enough. We grow disconnected from ourselves and leave our moral compass at the door. We forget things." She looked straight at her shitty camera and said, "Find a bosom to teethe on. Suckle yourself to sleep."

Why had Steph and Shereef not called me yet?

"We've passed the bingo!"

"I'll turn back, don't worry."

My back needed to be massaged by a bear, it ached as I leaned over the wheel. My knees hurt from pushing the foot pedals. I switched gears and relaxed on my seat. I pushed down on the gas. Mrs. Patrice had her seat belt on, so I switched gears again. She didn't say a word. I went 100 km/h in a 50, with a few sharp turns and one traffic light I didn't see. I'd worry later about whether there were cameras. I can't remember what Mrs. Patrice's expression was from the rear-view. I didn't really care to look. That morning's drive was just for me.

65

It had been almost ten hours since I'd last seen Jolene, and she still wasn't picking up any of my calls. Not a single response to my messages. She was somehow still able to carry on. Or was she dead? Had she killed herself in embarrassment? Did she choke on her fist because how does someone manage to sleep after having suddenly betrayed so many people?

I called Toni.

"I couldn't sleep," she said, her voice faint from my speakers.

"I can't think." I could hear her start to speak, but then she stopped. She usually had sound advice, her voice always one of reason.

"Did you speak to Jolene?" she asked.

"She won't answer my calls."

Toni sighed. We stayed on the phone together for a few minutes in silence, before I said I had to go.

The blackberry bushes around Doo Wop were trampled. Thorny vines were left snapped and lay on the ground like road spikes. Police tape gartered the perimeter, and a giant banner was plastered on the metal door: *Temporarily Closed*.

My phone rang.

"Stephanie!"

"Hey, babe. I just got home. They finally let me go after questioning."

"And Shereef?"

"They're keeping him in custody on"—she took a deep breath—"suspicion of terrorism."

"Fuck."

"They've sent a bunch of people to detention centers. I give it a few days before they're deported."

"I should've known, Steph. I didn't think that—"

"I know, babe. It's not your fault . . . I'm really tired, though, so let's speak later. I love you, D."

I drove to the garage.

The lion graffiti painted on Shereef's shop doors was more spectacular in the daylight. A sign was taped by the handle: *Open at 3pm, sorry for the inconvenience.* I called Jolene throughout the entire day, in between all of my rides. Why was she ignoring me? Didn't she want to explain to me how she saw her actions as justified? Why couldn't we just talk? It was common knowledge by now that good communication builds stronger relationships; how didn't she know such a basic fact? Surely her therapist was better than mine—or was she throwing all her money away? Was it all a lie? All I wanted to know was why?

66

If you can't afford a gym membership or don't have weights at home, you can work out using bedsheets. Take two sheets and tie a knot on one end of each. Hang them from the top of a sturdy door that you can properly shut. Keep the door shut with the knots on the other side. The sheets become your cables. You can pull, balance, and stretch using your own body weight in different positions and angles. We didn't have enough spare sheets at home for me to try this nifty hack, and I really wanted to.

"Got any hair clips lying around? If you take them apart right, the metal resembles handcuff shims. Want to learn how to escape?" The video I watched was titled "How to Escape from Being Tied Up in 5 Different Ways, Including Being Handcuffed." It had had three million views last month and four million that evening. I sat on my bench, watching on my laptop while I did some bicep curls. Every now and then I looked in the mirror to size myself up, thinking, I could have won a fight with the second passenger I'd had that day, but probably not the third, who stood around six foot two and had biceps the size of my head. Passenger 6, that would've been a fun fight to watch. Pay-per-view special, if that was still a thing.

"Zip ties are simple. It's all about force and position. From my hands this high, I'll pull down to my chest. It'll snap and voilà, I'll be free. You ready to see this, guys?" My biceps and triceps were getting more toned and with every curl I was hypnotized by how my muscles tensed. The lamp was on, but the glare from my laptop lit the room more. My hair was pulled back and my body was sweaty. I was easily becoming the new face of fitness; rough, not so cut, tough from the inside, no photo edits, please. I noticed that I had bags under my eyes, and I resembled Amma in a flashing second which threw me off a bit. In front of the mirror, flexing, my body was unlike it had ever been before. It wasn't vanity but I was in awe of how much I had pushed myself to build this strength, despite all that had been thrown at me. I laughed with my tongue out, looking dead in my own eyes. "You're a fucking badass with guns to match. You got this." I licked my lips. "I don't care if you think I'm sexy or not. I like cheese. So what? Forget all that. Don't stare at my arms. I want to know your intentions. Tell me who you really are." My hands caressed my arms. My chest was looking stronger too, so I did that thing we see men do—I tweaked one tit then the other, though in most of my attempts I felt my shoulders move too much. I cracked my knuckles, probably because I missed Shereef, then I jabbed: one punch, two punches, three. I reached into my back pocket. Fuck, why didn't I have a hairpin in there? "If you don't speak, I'm going to have to make you. Do you want to see what I can do? Yeah? Come on, let me show you something."

67

I made dinner and fed Amma. I put a butter knife up my sleeve, and two hairpins I'd taken out of Amma's hair in my back pocket. I'd wiped them both clean. Growing up, we'd had those cheap door locks, the kind that could be opened with a hairpin and a little jiggle. Butter knives worked well for some, but credit cards never worked as easy as they did in the movies. In any case, I had my switchblade in the glove compartment. Outside, the night was cool on my skin. I wanted to bottle this feeling.

I didn't know at what time it started, only that on Saturdays Jo had book club, where she joined a bunch of people to talk about recent bestsellers. Narratives about women who drank wine as they leered out their front windows to watch their sexy immigrant gardener. Crime thrillers that pathologized the choices of a maverick detective wasting his good looks and charm for the supposed greater good in a spine-chilling tale of copaganda. The ends justify the means. At least, that's what I imagined they were reading. I hadn't had the time to read a book in a while.

Jo's street was quiet. There was a man wheeling out

his garbage bin to the drive while smoking a cigar. What a life he must live. I waited for him to go inside, studying his front garden to kill time. On his lawn, there was an ornate scene made up of garden gnomes. One, which was wearing a green cap, held an empty pie tin, and another, with a blue cap, had pie all over its face. Why would he keep something so tacky on perfectly green grass? The coast was clear. Stepping out of my car, I kicked a gnome, snapping its head off, and then headed straight to Jolene's drive.

I started with the hairpins. I bent one end and straightened the other, poking around for a click, click. But Jolene had this lock that was probably a Grade 1 dead bolt. They weren't what I was used to jiggling through. I got my butter knife out but honestly, what was I thinking? From the trunk I got out my crowbar, looking around the street for peeping Toms and Sallys who might have the cops on speed dial. The crack of the door was too thin for the flat edge of my crowbar. I cussed, and wished I was made of gas.

"Excuse me." No one was to either side of me. "Hey, I'm over here." I discreetly concealed the metal to my side, and followed the voice, the footsteps hitting the pavement, a type of plimsolls, I imagined.

"What?"

"I'm still waiting for my Indian food."

"So?"

"Maybe you're delivering it to the wrong person?"

"Maybe I don't deliver food."

"Well, you don't have to be rude." The woman rolled her eyes and walked off. Before I could start prying Jolene's door again, a car passed by on the street. My legs hurt from crouching; my quads were still sore from my last lower-body workout. If I got a penny for every hour I'd ever waited, I'd be a rich little fucker. I realized that maybe it would be best to think like Jolene, WWJD. Jo believed in the universe and all things wonderful. Jo believed in a world with hopes and possibilities for everyone in equal measure. Think it, and it will manifest into something glorious in a single second. Door, door. Open, door. Open. I turned the handle. You wouldn't believe it, but the door was unlocked all along. She had said her door was always open, but I didn't think it actually was. Imagine feeling that safe?

From the moody summer night, with one step into her home I was in a magazine. There was a fireplace (although it was filled with dried flowers), a fur rug and a rattan rocking chair. Dotted around what I assumed was the living room, there were large palm plants and succulents. A cactus in the corner with a single purple flower in perfect bloom. On the leather couch, there were pillows that called to me, *"Come, be Goldilocks."* I sat down. I lay down. It felt just right. On the mantel were photos all lined up without a single speck of dust on a single frame. There was the happy Christmas-card family: mother, father. A brother? A sister? I'd thought she was an only child. Who were the others that looked so similar? There were pictures of Jo with her friends on vacation where the sun was high and the sky so blue. I recognized some of the faces from the fundraiser. The woman with the pink blouse, Kat, Sher—the woman who went Brown for no frowns, so nasty in bed. And there was Jolene with her friend who made maqluba and the entire Diversity-Is-All-We-Need gang.

The kitchen might as well have been a set for a food channel, hosted by a young, healthy, no-gimmicks bread girl or something. She makes sourdough, babka, croissants, and her own cheese. Fancy, yet wholesome. Equipped with a double oven that clearly had never been used. A fruit bowl full of tropical and local fruits adorned with fair-trade stickers. I didn't realize a youth worker could ever dream of living a life like this, fresh off the pages of my imagination.

I walked through to the hallway and I was in a museum. The floor had a rustic creak but was a new installation. How many holidays had she been on, and who put in all of these shelves for such an "exotic" souvenir collection? The walls had texture before they were smooth again; I ran my hands over them. I went to the bedroom and it smelled of cotton, wicker, and a beach breeze. The bed was comfortable—I could've slept and never had nightmares on that sturdy of a mattress—and on top of it was a duvet in a cover with a thread count that felt like cashmere. I left the sheets undone. Where did she get all those paintings from? Where were all her rugs made? I took my socks off (obviously despite breaking in I had still taken my shoes off at the door) so I could feel the softness of each rug on the soles of my feet.

In the bathroom, the shades of lipstick Jolene had could cover an entire canvas with multiple strokes. I put one on and I kissed and I kissed, leaving deep red smooches on the mirror. From the closet, I took the cleanest pair of running shoes she had, even though her feet are half a size smaller than mine, then I found a cashmere sweater for Steph and a paisley bandanna-styled camisole for Toni that I knew she'd love in Jolene's closet, but in any one of ours would be more "hood." I unrolled her yoga mat and lay on top of it with my eyes closed. My heart beat softly as I imagined I was home and she was downstairs trying out a whipped goat cheese and tahini recipe she'd found in the weekend papers.

I got up and walked through the hallway. The linen closet proved that she could fold both a flat and somehow a fitted sheet into perfect squares. I took two of each. In the kitchen, I looked in the fridge, taking a sip of kombucha that I then spat back in the bottle. How do people even drink that stuff? It tasted like an armpit. On her alcohol trolley—because she had her own alcohol trolley—I found a bottle of champagne, the same brand she'd brought on our picnic. I popped the cork, took a swig, licked the rim, and left the house wondering if, when she returned, she'd feel me.

68

Since Jo wasn't home, I drove by the Mademoiselle Ethiopia Café where she had said her book club was held. From the outside, the inside looked warm. There were only happy faces sipping earth's syrup while eating scones and muffins stuffed with quinoa and sweet potatoes.

She wasn't there.

Steph messaged me: *Toni made pound cake and curry goat, brought some for you and Amma. Watching Solitary Man with Amma now. Should I be worried? Michael Douglas makes her miss Appa more, right? Told her what happened btw . . . Shereef is still not home :(*

I drove to a few bookshops, in case I had misheard Jolene when she told me about her usual Saturday routine. She wasn't in any of them. Did she lie about her book club? Did she plan to send me on a wild goose chase? Was she even who she said she was?

I knew I was being intense, but I couldn't stop thinking about her, about what she'd said to me. What she'd done. What she'd maybe told the cops. I don't like being lied to—who the fuck does?

69

"I want you all to know that obsession is real. It's on the streets, it's in our homes, it's in our shopping malls. Everyone has an obsession."

Dr. Thelma Hermin Hesse's velvety voice matched her velvet blazer.

"You know I'm nothing but honest with my followers and I'm not afraid to share. Once upon a time ago, my obsession was bleach. I couldn't stop bleaching my toilet because I couldn't stand the smell of urine. But I've changed. I only bleach my toilet twice a week now. I have this kitchen towel, you see. A Bougie Extra Absorbent XL. I adore this product so much, I wish my mother had used it to clean my bottom when I was a baby. Mmm! It's so soft! So to deal with my obsession, into a single absorbent sheet I whispered all of my fears. Urine. Dirty ceramic. UTIs. Burning sensations! Within three miraculous days, I was resurrected from my obsessive thoughts and fears. I am brand new. Use my discount code for five percent off. Details are in the description box."

Dr. Thelma Hermin Hesse held a yellow-stained kitchen towel to her face, muffling her mic.

"You here for me?"

"Huh?" I'd forgotten I was waiting. "Pragash?"

"Cool." He got in my car and put his seat belt on.

I put my phone away and started the engine.

"Can you put the radio on?"

It was Sunday. Shereef wasn't home yet. Doo Wop was still closed, and would be for a while. I was thinking of Jolene's sadness and the polarity of her many faces. She had one and then another, and minute expressions in between. I knew that if I explained the magnitude of what she had done, she wouldn't understand, and I would be sucked of all my life trying to explain it to her. It was nearly 11:30 a.m. Mrs. Patrice was safe at home, knitting a pair of socks she said she was making for me.

I hated that I still had to go to work, when Shereef wasn't home yet, Doo Wop's undocumented workers were about to be deported to a random country none of them had ever stepped foot in, all while Jo was avoiding my calls, frolicking through life as though nothing had happened.

"Hello? The radio? Fucking forget it." Pragash (3.7 stars) tutted and put his headphones on. Either the biggest insult or the greatest relief was when a passenger put their headphones on.

My next passenger was Candace (4.6 stars) who had the tiniest, pearl-like teeth. She was a taxidermist, she said, and at night she prowled the city in search of carcasses. "For me, it's about preservation. One day we're all going to die, and it would be nice to know, somehow, we'll be remembered. You can't stuff a human, though. Not yet at least." She smelled of mothballs and hurting skin.

Good old Derek was supposed to be my passenger after that, and I was desperate for the ping. "The driver with no accent who can't mind her own business. I'm canceling the ride," he said as soon as he saw me.

Then there was an Amy (4.9 stars) who had that look I like. Goth girls with piercings and neo-traditional tattoos, one placed terribly on their thigh. They cut themselves in soft places. Their dildos were purple and they used them religiously on Friday nights. The yeastiness from the beer they drank could be smelled from between their legs.

After Amy there was a bald man, then a hairy man, a big woman, a small woman, a little boy who I hoped was okay. Something about him gave off neglect and hunger. I gave him five bucks and canceled his fare, having made $68 before deductions. Then after wandering and waiting for pings, I saw her.

My hands started shaking. If my heart rate was usually ninety beats per minute it was one hundred and eighty then. The cream of the crop—standing five foot seven with long legs, square shoulders, and without a real care in the world—was right there, not too far in front of me. She was outside a food truck that wasn't mine, holding more tacos than she could eat.

We had to have a conversation. At the very least we could find closure. I needed to hear her point of view. Dr. Thelma Hermin Hesse would be proud.

I parked on the side of the curb, watching Jolene. Her tacos were displayed on a table and she took a picture with her phone. The wind picked up her hair and the air around her stood still as she sat, picturesque, invoking all light to shine upon her. Why did she have ten tacos? Who was she messaging on her phone? I looked at mine and saw that Mrs. Patrice had sent me a picture of a half-knitted sock. I decided I'd call Jolene and wait for her face to react to my call. She looked up and around, surveying the space ahead, not even noticing my car. Or did she? She pressed "end." I clenched my teeth, and bit down too hard on my lips. She really didn't know what she'd done that night. How did she not get it? Did she even care?

I wanted to get out of the car, knowing it wasn't the right thing to do; I wouldn't allow myself to snap, but Jolene was Jolene and I am who I am. We had both made horrible choices.

But then my phone pinged with a new ride, and by the time I looked up again, she was already gone.

70

The ping was the start of a jackpot. Airport runs came through back-to-back and they brought the most money. Every passenger was flying away from this hell-hole and maybe they'd saved up for months to do so. They had surely counted down the days. They could be different where they'd fly to, pretending their destination was their true life. They'd sip margaritas at eight in the morning and wear clothes they'd pack away as soon as they returned. They'd feel happiness, but in brief bursts the realization that it was all just a mirage and they were only tourists would poke their bubble. I picked up one, dropped them off and then got a ping while at the airport, waiting only four minutes in the queue. I dropped those passengers off and got a ping for an airport run five minutes from that destination. Safely dropped off that passenger before getting another ping to the airport again. My tank was nearing empty.

My passenger was dressed in black and her suitcase was yellow. I wished it was mine.

"Let me help you with that." I got out and lifted her luggage effortlessly though it was "heavy," probably fifty-five pounds. "It's definitely over, if fifty is your limit."

"Sure. I don't really care."

I got in the car and started the engine. "Going somewhere nice?"

"My dad's funeral. My film premiere is this week, but I have to be in mourning for forty days."

"Probably longer."

"Excuse me?"

"I'm sorry for your loss."

"It's like he waited to die right when my career was about to take off. Ahh, my fucking life!" Angry Wannabe Star stared out the window, grinding her teeth. I thought how if I hadn't worked the night Appa died, maybe I could've picked him up from his shift before his heart stopped. Maybe if he'd known I was going to be there, it would've forced him to leave on time. I could've told him that another cook could fry up that beef. That it would taste just as good, even though we both would've known that was a lie. But I knew that at least Appa left his body doing what he loved. If I was going to die, I had one wish. Please, don't let me go behind the wheel of this car. Not on RideShare's dime. They'd charge Amma to collect my body.

I pulled up into departures, looking at the woman in my rear-view sitting miserable in my backseat. On the app it said I'd be paid $32 for the ride.

"How much is this drive costing you?" I asked her, watching her smirk.

"Obviously, it's your lucky day. It's $120 and that's ridiculous."

"Yeah, that is ridiculous," I mumbled gripping onto my wheel. I drove snug against the curb, parked the car, jumped out, and grabbed her yellow suitcase. Angry Wannabe Star in her neatly ironed black shirt and slacks, her eyebrows carefully combed with styling gel, stood with her shoulders back and I knew she had at least five-digits-decimal-two places in her bank account, question-able how much was in her savings.

"What does your mom do?" I asked, standing in front of her.

"She's a lawyer in New York City," she said, looking down at her phone.

"So she makes good money?"

"Yeah. And?"

"Then I'm sure you'll be just fine."

I got in my car and my windows were up so I couldn't hear her shouting at me from outside. Airports are cha-otic. I looked through Dr. H.'s video playlist, searching for validation, scrolling through her collection of heal-ing. The sweat on my fingers left a trace on my screen. I clicked on "Forgiveness and Regrets." I skipped through the first few minutes. White cat was on Dr. H.'s lap.

"We are bound to make mistakes. People are very sensi-tive. They need our help and we need each other. I called my Indian neighbor the P-word once, and she came over with a pot of tea and explained to me that that was offensive. She was Hindu, not Pakistani. I can forgive myself for my mis-takes. I can forgive her for her sensitivities. What's going on out there, we can fix together. This fine bottle in my hand

is The Fight. A new brand of water that will change our world. Use my code for ten percent off, links are all in the description box. Take a sip, breathe, and kiss a stranger on the lips. Don't forget, friends, like and subscribe, hit that bell so you're notified when the doctor is in. Let's be the change and keep hydrated."

I logged out; it was time to go home.

71

The cops were in our driveway and I wondered what lies were being spun about that night at Doo Wop. Shereef was still in custody, but maybe he had said something. He wouldn't have, though, and if he had, there was nothing to say about me. I knew Steph and Toni were safe because we had messaged each other. I thought of every other person on my street—maybe someone got shot? Then I realized it could've been Amma. She'd finally gone bananas and why was I not good enough to her? Did the wrong person think she was crazy and threatening? That she was illegal because her English didn't sound like English in their ears? Was it my speeding? Toni had said I was lucky I hadn't gotten stopped for it yet. But when you're a driver you know where the cameras are. Besides, I only drove fast when there were no people around. At least, I'd like to think so. As much as most people didn't want to hear it, the police were people too. Stupid people. Superfluous people. Power-crazed and missing half a brain, they were once children that bullied or got bullied. I stepped out of my car casually, wondering how much time I could get for grievous bodily on a fucking garden gnome.

Two officers waited in their cruiser. One looked like a fawn, the other was more experienced. Maybe he was a hog in a past life.

"Can I help you?" I rounded my words, code-switching as quick as my switchblade flicks open.

"Are you Dame-a, Damien-nee. Krish-na. Kris-ha—"

I stopped him, despite how entertaining it was watching him struggle. English letters spiced with island flavor. "I'm sorry, who?"

He sighed as if reading my name was the hardest thing he'd ever done. He took a breath and tried again. "Dam-ah-nye. Kris-ha. Kris-shan—"

Beads of sweat cumulated on the Fawn's forehead. I wanted to grab his face and spit in his mouth, saying, "Tell me how much you like it spicy?" I'd kick him in the balls. His partner came over and grabbed the paper from his hands. I was getting bored.

"Damani Krishanthan, you mean?"

"That's what I said."

"Sure, that's me. How can I help you, Officers?"

"We got a complaint and we don't want things to get messy."

"Messy? What do you mean?"

"I mean—"

"Surely you don't mind if some things get messy?"

The Fawn was like a virgin, seduced for the very first time. His mouth opened and I could tell the crack on his bottom lip hurt. His Adam's apple shifted when he gulped. His hands were now in his pockets, fingers scratching his inner thighs. The mature officer stopped him from even trying to speak anymore.

"Listen, sweetheart. Are you sure you've been on your best behavior?" His question made me see red, just a little.

"I don't know, are you fucking Santa? I'm so sorry. I shouldn't be swearing at you. I'm on my period. You know . . ." The things we have to say to people we couldn't care less about just to keep ourselves out of trouble.

"Oh, yeah. It's that time, is it? I've got a wife and three daughters. You don't have to tell me about it. It gets intense at our house. And it all happens at the same time. It's incredible. Lots of pads and crying. It's uncomfortable to watch." What. A. Fucking. Moron. He put a finger in his ear and gyrated it profusely. I wondered if a mosquito had bitten his brain.

"You know what I'm talking about, then. I'll go inside now and make a hot-water bottle for myself."

"All right, dear, you have a good night. Sorry to have bothered you."

"What the . . . ? John? What about the warning?"

"Ah, sugar. I was trying to be personable. You remember our training—build trust in diverse communities. Speak to the people. Open up a little. Share."

"Sarge, she's walking away."

"They call us pigs in this area, ya know."

"John."

"It's important to understand the method, Bill! You'll thank me when you've done as much time as I have. Young lady!" he called. I had only taken a few steps because I wanted to hear what they were saying; their conversation was nothing like the dialogue in those police dramas. "All right, before you take care of yourself, there's something you have to do for us. They've asked us to come down here to follow up on a lead. Apparently you were at the Doo Wop on the night of our counter-terrorism operation there."

I swallowed and smiled. Play dumber seemed to be working.

"I don't know what you're talking about. The Doo What . . . ?"

". . . We have been shown a call log by a Miss Jolene Marie Barnett-Smith. By the looks of it, this could be harassment, and that's a crime. Now, I know this sounds upsetting—luckily she didn't want to file a formal complaint—but we agreed to come down here and have a word. To avoid this escalating, it's best you keep away from Miss Barnett-Smith . . ."

Shit. Were they tapping my phone?

How many fridges did Jolene have in her summer house? How did her parents make enough money for her to live so comfortably without paying rent? She didn't tell me her secrets while I was suffocating on Amma and Appa's debt, my own, and the shit she suddenly threw at me. How did she get the police to come to my house, when Stephanie struggled to have an officer show up when her ex stole their TV? Toni was even told to calm down when a man grabbed her on the street. Jolene knew that if I got anything like a warning I wouldn't be able to drive anymore. If I wasn't driving, I wasn't working until I could find another job. Did she really want to hurt me that bad?

"I don't know where this is all coming from, Officers, but I can assure you I'll stay away from . . . I'm sorry, who was it?"

"Jolene Marie Barnett-Smith."

"Sure, I'll stay away from her even though I'm not sure who she is. I think there might be something going on with the phone network—all these riots, you know? What was her name again? It was pretty long and when I have my period everything goes fuzzy."

"Jolene Marie—"

"You know what, forget it."

"All right, dear. Anything we can do for you? We're here to serve and protect."

"Of course you are," I reassured. "You think maybe someone's mistaken me for someone else, though? You know that happens sometimes."

"No, we don't make mistakes like that."

"With all due respect, you guys can't tell us *all* apart, can you? No need to answer. I mean, you both look the same to me, too." I waited for their reaction and then I cackled. I swung my head back and let the laughs stumble out until they rolled. The officers laughed slowly too, then with gusto, and soon all three of us were cracking up like we were best friends forever, with bracelets to prove it. "All right, thanks for your time. Bye now. You two have a good night. Stay out of trouble." I started walking away.

"All right, sweetheart, you get that hot-water bottle going."

"No, John. Don't," whispered the Fawn, shaking his head in embarrassment. His hands were digging at his briefs through his thick trousers.

"You boys want to come in? Have some coffee? I won't poison you, I promise." There I was, losing all control.

"Excuse me?" The Fawn was suddenly on edge as if he'd remembered which part of the city he was in, and he crossed his arms to exude his authority.

"Just practicing some material, Officer sirs. I'm an aspiring comedian. Urban writer. Can't you tell?" I walked towards our door then turned around and waved, smiling with all my teeth.

72

On the kitchen table were overdue bills laid out and ready to be decoupaged onto the faux wood. Amma's bank balance, minus and in the red. Her credit card bills where money was used to pay other bills with numbers that never decreased. Thank you, interest. There were four final notices, one urgent, and a warning of eviction. I could plaster them, seal it, and sell it for two hundred dollars. *Have a Seat at My Table*, I'd call the piece. Appa and I had built this kitchen together when the house was ours, and the plan had been that someday the entire basement would be just mine. I opened the refrigerator and could see straight to the condensation on the back. Water dropped onto a ratty bag of wilted spinach. I had to go to the grocery store but my head hurt and it was late. I took some frozen chicken from the freezer and left it out to thaw.

"Damani."

"I know, Ma."

"What do you know? You see the table?"

"Yes, I saw the table."

"We have no more bananas."

In the fruit bowl there was a lemon with a silver dust-ing of mold in the dimples of its skin. There were a few drying plums that were practically prunes, and chil-ies that had shriveled in disgust. I knew then there was something I had to do.

73

In the bathroom there were clippers. I plugged them in. My reflection looked too familiar. I looked too kind. My hair was long because that's how Appa used to love it. "It's just like my mother's was," he had said. But my long hair made me look as though you could mess with me. You could grab it, pull me down to the ground, and put your foot on my face. You could stuff my hair in my mouth and call me pretty. I didn't need anyone to ever have that much leverage over me.

I found a pair of scissors in the drawer and cut off a few chunks which piled on the floor. I laughed a bit, because I looked incredible with each blunt cut and all the uneven ends. The person Jolene knew wasn't me anymore. At least, I wasn't the person she thought I was. I pressed the clippers to the side of my head and pushed hard upwards. The vibration buzzed in my ear and massaged my brain. Shorter strands dusted my cheeks, my ears, and my chest. They didn't want to leave me. Then I did the other side, leaving a landing in the middle. My head became my pussy's doppelgänger. I was better than nineties chic. I cut bits from the top, so I didn't look too raggedy, but there was something missing. My eyes weren't sparkling yet. In the cupboard, there was peroxide I had from the time I bleached Stephanie's hair. I lathered my head with it and waited.

Growing up, I never had dolls that resembled me. I used to cut all their hair off to see if there was a patch of skin that looked like mine underneath. I wonder what that actually did to my subconscious. I rinsed out the chemicals before they started to burn my scalp.

I had seen people chopping their hair off in the movies in an attempt to show us that the character was losing control and about to do something terrible. I had cut my own hair before. Granted, for me it started with just my bangs and then it was bits at the back. Then it was a shaved undercut that no one could see. This was what people I knew did when they couldn't afford to go to the salon, or when they didn't want to just cut it themselves or splurge hundreds of dollars they didn't have to feel a little bit of something good. The new person looking back at me in the mirror, though, that person was me. I finally saw myself as I was. I had full control.

74

Most people assume biceps give the arm that jacked look, but the biceps is a small muscle. It's all about building the triceps for a full arm. The dumbbell was heavy in my hand. In full concentration, I performed a tricep kickback, watching the muscle bulge in the mirror. The lamp was on and the tube light flickered until it fizzled and then went out completely. A shadow was cast on my face and I was the darkness, hiding from a world that couldn't ever truly love me. My tongue traced my teeth and I couldn't stop smiling because my God, I was handsome. I put the weight down and jabbed towards my reflection.

I had taken a mixed martial arts class some years ago before it got too expensive. Hear me say it now, everyone should learn how to fight because in doing so, you learn when not to fight; but maybe after all of this you won't take me so seriously anymore. I did a sequence: jab, cross, jab, hook, uppercut, over and over again until I couldn't breathe. I switched stances and did the same with my right leg forward, adding five roundhouse kicks and five teep kicks. My foot was aligned perfectly on my imaginary opponent's chest. In the dark, with our landlord's footsteps amplifying above me and the sounds of my neighborhood getting ready for bed, I dove towards the mirror, kissing my lips and leaving wet smears on the glass. I stood back, changing stances, feeling my new look.

"You want to get a little closer? Kiss my lips and tell me something. Tell me what I don't want to hear." To finish my workout and for one final pump, I held one of Jolene's soft sheets in each of my hands, which now hung from the top of my closed bedroom door. Leaning back, I pulled myself forward to complete a row, smelling her laundry detergent as I sank into each rep. I was a woman who wasn't going to take it anymore because I swear, I have taken so much already.

75

I switched gears and the night blurred past me, neon lights, red, amber, green, and a watery black that streaked into spilled ink. My windows were down and the wind blew through my short hair and along my freshly exposed scalp. I could hear chanting coming from somewhere in the city. My body felt strong and I wanted to break things. Full speed, I was coming for her.

76

There are people out there who believe we have been implanted with chips so that Big Brother knows where we are, what we're buying, and who we lie in bed with. When really, all of that information is pretty much in our phones. Jolene was an easy stakeout because she shared her entire schedule with me, just once, and that was enough. The thing about drivers is, we remember everything. The roadblocks, the side streets, the passengers we don't want to drive around twice. Maybe our connection was deeper than we had both realized it could ever be. We were polar opposites, each other's north and south and the magnetic force that brought us together, guided me to her, and her to me. Every. Single. Time.

I didn't have to wait outside Jolene's house for long. The door opened and she had on a Lycra set, a green one this time, with her earbuds snug in each ear even though it was way too late to be careless. I sank further down into my seat, grateful for the anonymity that this job had taught me. It was Sunday night, of course she was going out for her run. She didn't even bother to look around and notice my car, or she didn't care that I was right there, watching. The pavement practically cushioned her feet, nothing was allowed to hurt her. I watched Jolene disappear into the night.

My intention on driving to her place, not realizing that she jogged so late, was to bang on her door, storm into the house, sit with her on the couch and demand answers. But seeing her trot along enraged me.

The titanium bat I had in the trunk was signed by Joe Carter. It was a fake of the one I imagined he swung to win the 1993 World Series. Thirty years later, the bat still fit snug in my hands.

The new *Good Vibes Only* placard that hung on her door was obnoxious. In her front window, my reflection was as clear as the one I saw in my own mirror. Teeth clenched, grip tight, my shoulder snapped as I pulled the bat behind me. I could see myself swinging using all my power; the window shattering in a single blow as each bit of cracked glass fell piece by piece onto the ground with the gorgeous sound of destruction. I pulled the bat from over my shoulder and swung, but I stopped mid-extension. I couldn't do it. I wouldn't give Jolene the satisfaction and what would her broken window actually achieve? I ran back to my car, hearing the imaginary crunch of shards under my feet.

77

There was a switchblade in the glove compartment, but I already told you that. I put it in my back pocket. The tire iron was under my seat and my aviators were on the dashboard. The rope, bat, and duct tape were still in the trunk. There was no time to get distracted.

I was now parked beside a line of trash cans where it smelled of old pricey pizza and stale vinegar, outside the track close to Jolene's house. Floodlights shone, lighting up each lane so every granule of the rubbery all-weather running track could be felt from far away. Squishy and comfortable on the sole. I waited and waited, trusting in Jolene's vanity, because she only ran to maintain her physique. After a few minutes or so, she came galloping along with her headphones still on because of course she didn't really worry about her safety in this area. I put on my shades. It didn't matter that it was dark. I had a bandanna in my pocket. Her Lycra set was seamless and reflective; I couldn't miss her even if I tried. I waited for her to round the corner—I thought it was best if she ran a bit more so she would tire herself out. With my eyes still on her, I moved the car a little closer to watch her run 100 meters, and then another, before I got out of the car and stretched.

Jolene had done a lap and a half on the 400-meter track, and just before she made it to 800 meters I ran towards the lane beside her. No indicators, no warning, no fear. Though she was fast, she was slowing down. I had speed and was running full throttle but no way could I run for too long. Our feet were almost silent on the incredible track ground, another sign that her property tax was probably more than our rent. My shades slid on my nose, so I put them in my pocket. Aviators weren't designed for sprinting. Jolene was finally easing into a jog. Just a little more and I would've been right behind her. Singing off tune to whatever she was listening to, her strides shortened with each step.

I know it wasn't my finest hour, I'll admit it. But since she was making all of this so difficult, I had to do something quick. I wasn't a sheep as she played me out to be. I had to scare her. Just a little. Staring at her back, I leaped forward, tackling her to the ground.

"What the heck!" She fell, slipping on all fours, desperate to slide away. "I won't let you hurt me." She was struggling with her words.

"Are you fucking kidding me?" I said, looking down at her, pinned below me.

"Damani?" I didn't know what to say. In good habit, I smiled, showing off all of my teeth. "Your hair?"

"Do you like it?"

"Not really," she confessed, and in her blunt response my feelings were hurt. Again. "You're not supposed to be near me. I need to figure things out."

"*You* need to figure things out? Shereef is in custody and he won the most kind award in high school! People who made a life here are getting deported and Doo Wop is shut down. You owe *us* an explanation."

"I don't owe you anything, Damani," she said, crushing me even more. "You need to get off of me or—"

I was once stabbed in the flank while crossing the street. My body quickly collapsed and the first thing I thought of was whether I'd signed out from my shift at the sandwich shop I worked at. My manager had said we wouldn't get paid if we didn't sign in and out right, even if we started on time and worked our entire shift. It took six stitches and some bed rest to make me all better again. But ever since, if the clock struck a certain chord and I felt threatened, instinctively I'd flip out my switchblade.

The edge of the knife was to Jolene's neck. The reverberation of her heartbeat tapped my thigh and in that split nanosecond, I wanted to kiss her. She screamed, not out of fear so much as an expression of adrenaline and in an incredible swing of movement that she performed without so much as a thought, she headbutted me. Her head was heavy. I remember how fervent her eyes were and I knew that when she was determined, she was unstoppable. She had been the goddess Apate staring right at me. I fell to the ground, holding my head. I landed on my back. My eyes were closed from the bright spaceship lights above.

Using every ounce of power I had, I stood up and looked Jolene in the eyes, because she was still standing in front of me as if she cared that maybe she'd caused me some pain. She looked aghast. We were strangers for those seconds, which made it easier to push her back down to the ground again. I leaped forward and grabbed her torso. What can I say? I've got muscles I know how to use. Grabbing her by the wrist, I dragged her a few feet before she sank her teeth in my hand. I tripped like an idiot who couldn't tie her own shoelaces and fell shamefully to the ground again. Jolene looked at my face and used the moment to her advantage. She ran off, not even bothering to look over her shoulder, leaving me alone in the night.

I lay on the ground, facing the sky, waiting for my composure to check in; then I got up with my dignity, brushed my clothes of any dirt and grass, and walked towards my car. It was an "In the Air Tonight" sort of night. I cranked up the volume, noticing just how worn the buttons on the radio were. I played Phil Collins as loud as I could while I reclined in my seat. When the song finished, I replayed it three more times. I couldn't let Jolene just walk away from me again. Not after what she had done.

78

The television was on. It was closer to day than it was to any night. I'd spent hours driving around. Amma was in the kitchen. The room smelled moldy. My mother's eyes never leave me, even when I am out of her sight. When I stare into them I can practically feel the ground shake. She looked at my hair before she actually looked at me.

"This is not good."

"I know, Ma." I walked to my bedroom and lay in my bed with the clothes I wore outside. Black mold dotted the ceiling like stars. My body was weightless, having surrendered to my own fatigue. I knew that I would sleep.

79

When I woke up, only a few hours later, I was sure a part of me was sitting on my dresser, watching me with knowing eyes, telling me the day wouldn't be comparable to any I'd ever lived before. Amma had made oatmeal. I could smell the oats softening in the milk she made with coconut she'd grated and massaged in a bowl of water. I lay on my mattress for another few minutes with the covers over my head, feeling that part of me that was on the other side of the room, now on top of me, poking my left eye.

I'd woken up too late for Mrs. Patrice's bingo drop, and I hoped she was okay. I didn't want to work and give RideShare my dime in this rotten city but I had no choice. Like every day.

I stepped in the shower and ran the water warmer than usual. My body stiff under the trickling stream, my scalp not used to the exposure. Amma knocked on the door.

"Damani?"

"Yeah, Ma. I'll be out soon." I saw from the light that peeked under the door that she still stood there long after my response. I waited for her to walk away.

I went through my closet. I pulled a white shirt over my head, stepped into a pair of faded black jeans, and threw on Amma's old khaki-green chore coat. It still had the David's Cookies badge from the factory she'd worked at, sewn on the side with an Employee of the Month badge right underneath it.

When I finally got into my car, I settled down. This was my kingdom. My domain. The app could take what they wanted, but this was still mine.

I circled the block, hoping my phone would ping, but it didn't. My head throbbed. I'd slept, but not enough. The back of my throat was parched and the acid in my stomach rolled and splashed in sulphurous waves. People were blurs smearing my vision like streamers waving in the warm wind. I wanted to touch myself but I was too tired, and I only wanted to because the sleep I'd fall into after climax would have me descending into the bosom of the earth. Someone honked behind me and that was not the right thing for them to do. I stopped my car and stepped out. Vehicles passing by honked at me as if I was running straight into them. The culprit's window was tinted. I knocked with my fist, and he lowered it. His face was a shriveled scrotum, more from the sun than from age, and he had balanced large aviators on his nose. I remembered how Shereef once said that retired officers play undercover sometimes.

"There's rope hanging out from your trunk. Do you even have a license? I nearly crashed behind you." I wanted to bite his nose off. I wanted to make him dinner at his home, light him a cigar, then shit in his toilet. I wanted to feed him my shit for dessert.

"I didn't realize."

"Have you been drinking?"

"If I was drinking, why would I be driving?"

I looked at him, trying to appear truthful even though I was telling the truth. He shook his head.

"You people." He was almost smiling as he said it. What, you don't believe me? Go ahead, call me unreliable. I know it wasn't in my head.

80

I wasn't getting any pick-ups. Zero pings. So I went home to sleep. I knew enough about myself to know that sometimes sleep was the greatest medicine; time passes, moods stabilize, and in dreams we are somewhere better. My alarm didn't go off, or else I hadn't put it on. I tried counting how many hours I had slept for. I worked out how much money I'd potentially lost and realized I'd sacrificed my favorite treat, granola—the one with chocolate chips, almonds, and honey—double-ply toilet paper, and about a quarter of the water bill. The whiff of bleach and pine nearly scrubbed out my nostrils as I sat hearing a squeak over glass. Was Amma up and cleaning?

I checked my phone to find missed calls and texts from Toni and Steph: *Why aren't you answering? You good? Big protest tonight! Don't work late!*

A message from Mrs. Patrice: *What happened this morning?*

Then one from Shereef: *I'm home. Finally. We should meet. Try not to drive out tonight.*

I responded to him immediately: *I'm sorry, Shereef.*

He was quick with: *Why should you be sorry?*

I started to type: *I love you* in response, but then deleted it before deciding to send: *Because I should've known better.*

To which he responded: *You did nothing wrong.*

81

The city has jagged edges and it sits in my hand. It was five p.m. Earlier, I had put on the RideShare app, but there were no pings. I had hoped that while searching for Jo, I could make money along the way. I had to. Normally, I didn't have to wait too long for passengers, so I restarted my phone and tried again but it wouldn't sign into the app. I called Shereef.

"Yo! D."

"Your voice."

"I know, I'm alive."

"Terrorism, eh?"

"Apparently. No issues with RideShare yet. Hoping there's no investigation."

"Yeah," I sighed.

"How's Jolene?"

"She won't answer my calls."

Shereef grunted a tired laugh. We were silent for some time. "We'll talk more about it in person, yeah?"

"For sure."

"You going to come by?"

"Maybe late tonight? Trying to figure this out. I can't log in to my account."

"You get any tickets?"

"Not really."

"You okay? Want to meet now? Did they send you an email?"

"One second. I think they did."

"All right, sort it out, we'll meet up later."

I checked my emails and there it was. A message from them, the useless company. I was suspended until further notice. Suspicion of criminal activity. They would begin an investigation into my account.

I knew a driver who was still waiting for her sexual harassment claim to be investigated, and let me be clear she was the one who was harassed. And now here I was under surveillance because—well, I wasn't sure why. My suspension until further notice meant I couldn't work until they'd figured out if I was at fault for something that I'd apparently done.

Under a street lamp, a man played the tenor saxophone and I couldn't tell if it was because he had to or because he loved to. Either way I stood alone, watching him blow into his horn as the city carried on without us. Inside of my body, my pulse played a rolling drumbeat. My sight grew hazy and my body swayed, watching the man's fingers slide up and along his sax. He knew where to move and just how much to blow for the most perfect sound. I took a deep breath in to recenter. When there is a problem, there is a solution. There was no time to rest.

82

The bathroom, kitchen, and living room were spotless. I suddenly had a lot less work to do. Amma was sitting in the armchair with the television on. She looked different, so close to normal that you'd think Appa was on the toilet and when he'd finished they were going for their usual night walk. I didn't mention it because my teeth were clenched. How was I supposed to tell Amma that I couldn't make money anymore?

"You're not working tonight? We can watch a movie," said Amma, staring at my hair with her eyebrows furled.

"I came back to see if you're okay."

"Of course. I'm fine."

I sat down on the couch, slouching. I could feel Amma's stare. When I turned to look at her she glanced quickly back at the TV. "Toni said you didn't call her," she said. I stared at the screen. People with plastered grins were doing back-flips into complete dance numbers, enthused by a new flavor of gum. "She's bringing me a medicine ball, so I can exercise."

"That's nice of her." The television was too bright with flashing images, too loud with catchy jingles. The advertisements were over. After some time Amma said,

"I don't want you to stress, D. We have another final eviction notice. I'm going to make bread pudding. You want some?" She stood up, brushed her batik kaftan, and walked towards the kitchen. Her legs stiff and slow, she still moved with confidence.

The presenter speaking on the television was pretty and I hated seeing pretty on TV. I wished the stylist hadn't done her hair so neat. I wished the presenters we all had to look at on the evening news appeared as most of us were in the evening: cozy, worn, comfortable. It looked as if it hurt to be her under the stiff clothes she wore. And there I was judging her and not listening to what she actually had to say.

"*Large groups of demonstrators are protesting every-where, and the city is torn.*"

"*And we have got to stop these riots! It's completely unacceptable,*" said a man in a box above her shoulder.

"*How are any of them riots? What if someone actu-ally went out with Molotovs—?*" started a much younger woman sitting in a box underneath him.

"*So you're bringing weapons, then, are you?*" inter-rupted the man.

"*How? What? I didn't say that. Listen, it's evident in the streets that the government and our trust in the elite has failed so many groups of people. There are kids hungry. Black people are being wrongfully arrested. And we still don't know what happened to the two hundred people put in those cattle sheds!*"

"They were re-fitted!"

"I don't care! Women are being taken at night and the planet is literally burning. War criminals are leading our country, and the wealthy are making decisions for the working class. How is any of this acceptable?"

"This is what is wrong with your generation, young lady. You don't understand politics."

"Just stop talking. What we're seeing is that there is power in numbers, our struggles are interconnected. The system is failing us, and the state is responsible for that! It's our civil right to be out there."

"See! This is the rubbish we're forced to listen to! These are the loony leftists that want to see communism and socialism, all these fairy-tale ideas. It's not real life. Enough of it! And coming from people like you? You have got to be grateful for being here, young lady. This country has opened its doors for you. The vitriol we're forced to hear is what spreads the hate. It's this kind of paranoia that is infecting the youth—no, let me finish—into believing they ought to be some sort of social-justice warrior. There is no war to fight. There is no evil structure bot that must be destroyed. I woke up and that's as woke as I'll be. That's it! We had the best of times in this country, and if we let these lunatics out there take charge then we're destined for the worst. I'm tired of it," said the man.

"And your whole spiel isn't part of the propaganda protecting the elite? Who controls the media?"

The pretty woman wanted to go home and I finally saw

that in her eyes. She tried to calm the conversation and neutralize the two speakers—"let's agree to disagree." We all knew she was dreaming of running a hot bath.

"Are you going to tell me, Damani? I made food. I went outside. Tell me, D. Why did you cut your hair like that?" asked Amma from the kitchen.

"You don't like it?"

"It's scary."

"You're scared of everything, Ma."

Amma charged her way into the living room with a wooden spoon in her hand—I thought her knees would snap. The spoon, which was stained with turmeric, was pointing towards the tip of my nose. "You don't know what I've lived and seen, pillai." I looked at the end of the spoon, following Amma's arm to her face. Her skin was clear, without any dried smears of leftovers or any crumbs speckling her cheeks. Embarrassed by my stare and lack of reaction, she tutted, kissing her lips. On the television, the camera panned over the crowd in the city center. People were blowing horns at the camera; some wore party hats with brightly colored bunting around their necks. Face after face, fist upon fist, I found Jolene. There she was without a single regret. The camera loved her face as much as I did, and it zoomed in on her because she stood out in a crowd. Before Amma could even say a word, I'd grabbed my keys.

"That's the girl who came here. Damani? Damani!" shouted Amma as I slammed the door behind me.

83

I parked my car in a disused parking lot where shards of broken beer bottles made a green, black, and amber mosaic on the ground. Temporary fence panels were piled in a mess, completely forgotten about. Four were positioned to make a pen, inside of which were two plush toys—a blue grizzly bear and a green piglet—and a broken wooden rocking horse with a missing eye. A dirty off-white blanket had been left spread in the middle, and on it a pacifier, the nipple half-chewed, the tip bitten off. I put the handbrake on and switched the engine off, opposite a brick wall that was scribbled on with graffiti that read, **The Skyline Is on Fire** beside a giant penis with very distinct curly pubes on the scrotum. **Mr. Pee Pee wants money,** was written below the sac.

When I opened my car door I realized I had parked close to a hole. There was an opening in the concrete somehow, and growing from below was a type of shrub about a foot tall. It made me notice the many cracks in the pavement, and the weeds that managed to grow through them with a plan to overtake the entire city. The broken windows of the dilapidated office buildings surrounding the area were eyes winking directly at me, trying to lure me in through their front doors, where the ghosts of office workers lived and no one was allowed to enter. Even in this derelict state, some kids had tried to make the parking lot a haven for themselves. A stained mattress was leaning against the sides of a dumpster. I was sure that if anyone managed to slide down it with short-shorts, they were likely to contract an STI. *Wheee!* Right into an infection.

I opened my trunk and eyed my collection of items with admiration. There were still some sour-cherry candies in the pack I'd found. I threw some in my mouth, but it was too many at one time so I spat them on the ground. Red and green crystals coated in strings of spit looked like jewels on the concrete. I took out the roll of duct tape and even though I had a pair of scissors under the mat by my seat, I wanted to use my knife. I don't get to use it often enough. I pulled a strip and stuck it onto my bumper, then I cut it from the roll. Eyeing the size of the print on my license plate, the height a hair shorter than my index finger, the width a sliver off the nail of my baby finger, I carefully pulled the end of the tape taut and cut a thin piece to size. I stuck it precisely on my zero, so it was now an eight with one dash of matte silver. With the same attention, I cut another piece and put it on the zero on the front plate. I could pick up passengers myself. Fuck the company. I wasn't interested in advertising, but I wanted to be understood like anyone else out there.

I took out my spray paint and shook the can. The clicking sound of the ball bearing made me want to spray liquid out from my mouth in a gush of excitement. For whatever reason, in that instant I craved a bowl of ramen noodles that cost only one hundred and ten pennies. I wanted to pour that bowl on my head. I wiggled my fingers before positioning the can carefully. I sprayed T-A-X-I on the hood of my car, right where Jo and I had laid on it at the beach. I spray-painted the back as well, as best I could, single drops still dripping from the point of every letter. The city loved labels, so there was mine. I was a cab driver. I would drive you safely to wherever you needed to be. I was underrated but essential, the backbone to all that was thriving, and the people needed me just in the way that Jolene and I needed to talk.

Where was she? I was going to find her.

84

The people who were protesting moved as a tide through the street that night. Their chests rising and falling in unison as they chanted, building momentum with every one of their voices. The crowd was draped in banners ending with exclamation marks. Sometimes with three. On the main streets, a tapestry of felt tip and card flashed every second my wheels rolled an inch further.

Stop Deportation Flights
RAGE against INJUSTICE!
How Many Signs Do We Need—WE ARE FUCKED!!!

Down these main roads, vehicles could only pass when there was a parting in the sea of people. So every now and then police officers intervened to ensure traffic kept moving. I took a side road to maneuver around the congestion, still hearing the thunder of voices somewhere not too far behind.

I fiddled with my rear-view and carefully scanned my wing mirrors, hoping to pick Jolene out from the crowds. The way she stood, the way she hunched every now and then, the way she laughed. I flicked the radio on, then off immediately. I noticed my gas was near empty but I was sure I had just filled it. An icon on my dashboard lit, informing me I needed an oil change even though She-reef had already changed it. One thing after the next, it was destined to be one of those nights.

Keeping my eyes on the road, scanning every quadrant I passed, leaning over my steering wheel, I was close to giving up. About three squares of sidewalk away from me, a swarm of people who held procession torches were shouting a chant that was so inaudible I wondered why they wasted their breath. If only they could take a second to be in tune and in time with each other, but I think the rush of carrying fire down a city street makes those slight details irrelevant. Even if they matter. Shit was about to rain down and that night it wasn't going to be from the pigeons.

"Abolish the military! Stop killing Muslims! Black lives matter!" someone screamed into my passenger window before running off into another crowd flowing towards the center.

Where was Jolene?

A couple held each other on the side of the street ahead of me. I stopped my car opposite them.

"Want a lift?" I asked, shouting from my window. Con-fused, they studied my car and began laughing, shaking their heads before one of them raised their fist to the sky.

Of course, wherever there are people congregated, there will be cops on guard with shields and batons, and who knows what else in their pockets. Some of them had dogs. Some were on horses. They formed a phalanx around the people, and then just stood there, with no clue of what to do.

Drones hovered above the theatrics of the city. Slowly but surely, the crowd was heading towards the city center, and I followed. Before I turned a bend, I saw placards for the canceling of student debt, the canceling of all debt, and I realized that if my debt was wiped to zero, I would finally be able to answer my phone without putting on a different voice. *"Hullah? Who speakin'?"* Debt collectors too often called me on restricted numbers.

I debated turning back, but it was impossible with the traffic. I couldn't give up, but I wanted to. I kept going forward on what felt like a never-ending road to the end of the world, until the traffic was nearly clear. There was a left turn ahead where I could easily turn around. I put on my indicator. Tick. Tock. Tick. Tock.

And then I saw her. Jolene.

85

She was alone. She looked around as if she knew someone was watching her. It's not a nice feeling, is it? She had a sign and I wished I could've read it, but she held it close to her body, turned the other way. I drove closer because she was still too far for me to get out and walk. I wanted her to feel me before she saw me and by the way she looked around, I got the sense she knew I was near. I put a stick of gum in my mouth. My cologne was still in the glove compartment so I sprayed my wrists, rubbing them together. Gripping my steering wheel, I drove closer and stopped. She looked ahead and saw my car. Hearing the swarms of people, the buzzing of drones, and the thundering helicopters that now encircled above us. I smiled with my mouth open so she'd know I came in peace. She was beautiful—terrible, but beautiful. I put my hand up to wave, but when she realized it was me, she ran.

86

Jolene ran like a fucking horse. She took over the sidewalk, leaping over every crack. She looked behind her shoulder, Maradona-turning between pedestrians, then stopped at a light. Steadfast, she wouldn't let go of her sign, clinging to it as though it bore her truth and to lose it would be losing her purpose. I made out the words from where I was in the traffic watching her, enraged that she wasn't in my car. *We Need Love,* her sign read and I almost laughed.

I was glad I could keep up with her, driving parallel. I lowered the window some more and could hear demonstrators from a few blocks away crescendo even louder. This was one more of many summer nights we could have shared together. We could have been at her summer house. "Jo! We need to talk!" She looked back and stopped for a second. I sidled up to her, scraping the curb. Honks followed around me. Her expression in that instant was as I'd never seen it before. It seemed that she had more than forty-two facial muscles trying to tell me something. Why did she look at me like that? She ran faster. She ran on the road, unafraid of vehicles, unafraid to die. She cut off another car, and I saw my opportunity. I hit the gas to follow her.

I looked up to see where she was going.

The police station was ahead. People marched from the other side, their feet echoing, louder and louder. Even though the chanting was coming closer I swear I heard her fucking footsteps running to her God; she ran faster and faster, because fucking hell she was a horse that I should place bets on, and I had no choice but to show her that she wasn't shit compared to my B16A engine. I drove forward, switched gears, and pressed on the gas. I saw how my revolutions per minute pushed to the right. She looked at me over her shoulder. I pressed even harder on the gas and closed my eyes.

87

There was a hand on my shoulder. Smoke burst from the hood and into my car through the dashboard. My head had bled on my steering wheel because of course I didn't have air bags that worked like they were supposed to. There was a ring in my ears that wouldn't stop; I'd almost forgotten where I was. Under my nose was wet and warm and when I touched it, my fingers were stained red. The taste of iron filled my mouth.

"Are you okay?" Someone opened my door, letting the brisk air hit my face with a what-the-fuck-did-you-just-do.

"Get out. Get out quick. Can you run?"

"Someone help!"

"Shield the car!"

"Protect her!"

There were a few police officers on guard outside the station that I saw run towards me, before running back inside. The rest looked on, watching from the inside behind a protective shield of glass. I didn't know what was happening but she was there, an apparition in a police officer's arms. She was being comforted. I was still bleeding. There were people all around, running in my direction from every junction. I slipped out of my car and a column of demonstrators pushed forward past me, blocking my vehicle. My wing mirror was on the ground. I stumbled over detritus, feet, and disbelief. A woman grabbed me. "Get out of here. Run fast. We got you." Looking behind, protesters screamed and chanted in celebration. I saw some others in tears. The high-rises were a gate, cops that were on duty on the streets ran towards the back of the station. My car was being pushed by hordes of people who understood me. I was shoved towards safety, and Jolene was out of sight.

88

The day my parents were forced to sell their house and rent out their own basement, I had asked Appa why life was so unfair. He had said in the calmest of ways, "Because the greater the divide, the stronger the rule, chellam." Then he kissed my cheek and said, "This won't be for long." He could've just said it was because we came here broke, and we will probably die here broke, and that would've made more sense to me.

I ran until the cool night air gripped my lungs. I was far enough away. The sky seemed to fall on my back and I imagined the stars finding ways to nestle in my hair, reminding me I was born from its dust and from the dirt I stood on, where my ashes would one day rest before becoming stars again. I walked until I was ready to feel like I was choking again. I ran and ran, seeing Jo in my mind's eye. She was more than a damsel, she was an obstruction to our love and so much change. I missed my father who was beyond the greatest divide. I needed him to come back, just for a second. Just so I could say good-bye properly. Just so I could say, Thank you for working so damn hard even though I still have to.

"I can't do this," I screamed. No one was there to hear

me as the sound of my voice tapered off into the night. I felt myself losing myself and I wanted to go home but I didn't know where that was or what that felt like. I wanted to be in Hot Kitchen under the spell of fried deviled beef and island spices, watching my father living a different sort of life far from the back of the house. But I couldn't ever have that.

89

Our place was cleaner than usual. The sheets on Amma's mattress were made with straight edges as smooth as icing on a cake, and her pillows were fluffed so perfectly that if I was tiny enough I'd dive into them and suffocate on clean linen. She was sitting in the armchair still watching the news, but this time with a glass of wine in her hand. Someone was talking about an incident at the police station and a burning car. Amma was trying so hard to be the woman she was six months ago. She and Appa did all they could for me. Seeing her as she was now, her age appearing more and more on her skin and hair, her story written on the lines of her face, I cried like I had never cried before.

"Oh, my kunju," soothed Amma, getting up from her chair. I cried harder and louder, a bubble of snot forming in my nostril, yet she held me. I fell on my knees, holding her feet. I banged the floor with my fists. "Okay, Damani. Get it out, but people are sleeping upstairs."

"I don't care!"

Amma went to the kitchen.

"Okay, D., take it easy now." She had something in her hand as she returned.

"I'm so damn tired, Ma!"

From behind her back, she revealed a bag of chocolate almonds. Her face was mine, though she thought I looked more like my father. She knelt beside me and held my hard body with hers, still fragile.

"I'm here," I said in her ears, brushing her salt-and-pepper hair with my paw.

"Me too," she said. "Me too."

90

Cool Cat Boss Meow—What happened tonight is what needs to happen more often! Defund the Police!

PiersGordan78—Through violence? Come on!

Silent Lamb—Who was it though?

The Queen's Bandit—These left-wing radicals held the police station hostage! They are getting out of control! We need tighter legislation and more cops out there!

Shay on the Street—So far 202 demonstrators were arrested and charged for kidnapping and false imprisonment when the police chief ordered officers to stay inside! They are finding new ways to stop peaceful protests! #Justice #FreeAllPrisoners

Swifty Fingers—Peaceful? Did you not see the car that literally drove into the station?

SPEAK OUT 89—The station at central kept it low key. Elsewhere police used force against hundreds of protestors. Three children are in hospital. Injuries—so far 53 reported.

NO Means NOO—and two officers were beaten! Two broken ribs.

Yes and 99—@NOmeansNOO YES AND they were injured by other officers' batons. Did you see the video?

RadRed—Why didn't we all just occupy every police station?

Socrates467—Because we don't want to die!

HenrySucks—The police have been watching these idiots destroy our city for days! This was bound to happen.

Dreamy Eyes—Tonight we saw a movement! People Power!

Karen Kay Kay—Violence is not the answer. Violence against women? That is certainly not the answer.

Exterminate the Brootes43—This is all they ever wanted. The police are cowards now!

Everything Is Propaganda—@ExterminateTheBrootes43 you really don't get it, do u?

I See All Things—The loony leftists, the hippies, and the thugs. They're all causing mayhem, and my tax money will be used to clean up their mess. We need stronger leadership!

Unapologetic Boomer 69—@ISeeAllThings Exactly! These kids need to stop complaining. This is unacceptable. Find the terrorists and lock them all up!

Average Joe 75—Yes! Deport all terrorists! We need to protect our officers! #heroes

Call a Bill a Bill—Close our borders!

Young Cramps—Go back to your countries!

Siva23—You were in our countries first! We're here because you were there, mate.

Proud FAM—Not all colored people think that! I'm happy to be in this country. Just follow the rules, people. #notALLofUS #noteverythingisracist

Philosopher Pete—Why are brown people always drivers?

Trolling in your Dreams—Model minority my ass!

69er—Horny hour! Message me your tits and dicks.

Grace Keller (PhD)—Social media won't save us! Pray for Myanmar. A thread.

Real Talk Stacy—What was the point of tonight's events anyway? We need to stop the violence! Decolonize our revolutions!

Your Wife's Worst Nitemare—Follow me for funny facts. Fans Only for titties and ass whippings. Cream Pie Tuesdays. Don't tell your wife or add your wife. I'm waiting ;)

Starr—Facts are Facts. Black Lives STILL Matter.

No Names Here—Can we just take some time to reflect on what people in numbers can achieve together?! The oppressed will rise up! #together #TrueSolidarity

Future Thots—We need reform over revolution, you idiots.

Junior88—There will be no real change until we revolt. What a hero we saw today!

Malcolm65—We need love, is all over the papers. That love has to be revolutionary!

K. Starman—The sweet woman that psycho tried to kill may have been Jewish. We cannot support anti-Semitism. The terrorism must stop!

Say it Louder—From the river to the sea, Palestine will be free!

Anime Freakzz—I want to be that driver when I grow up!

King Charles8934—I want my country back!!

Grow Until Your Old—Garlic Scapes and Bae—Hi! We are Travis and Patrice. Tune in every Sunday afternoon for tips and tricks for growers. More spending on community gardens please. # No GMOs. SAVE OUR SEEDS.

Jo with Attitude—I'm not ready to make a public statement yet. But, I'm on here to ask for all your help. My friend needs us! Please donate what you can. Her mother is disabled and they both suffer with undiagnosed mental health issues. Come on folks! Donate!

Hyper101—@JoWithAttitude, show us your tits and you'll get more $$

Jo with Attitude—I will not be responding to any comments. I appreciate those of you supporting me and this great cause. I am still healing and recovering. #AllyBurnOut #solidarity #BLM

Angel Baby be Mine—What a role model, Jo! U R incredible!

91

Amma and I had fallen asleep on the carpet. I woke up, choking on a drop of spit that somehow disrupted my entire rhythm of breathing. My stomach churned. I knew the city was talking about me. The hush of whispers in my ears or Morse code tapping on the window. I anticipated there would be a knock on the door soon. I didn't want to let Amma go because I knew I might never see her again. How many years could I get for driving in a rage of love and anger? I wondered if I had been shot. Maybe the bullet was lodged so deep I couldn't feel it. I was lucky to be alive. A chocolate almond had melted in my hand. The saltiness of my sweat, dried blood and dirt coated my tongue with the sweetness of the chocolate when I licked my palm. The taste woke up my senses and I could feel the knot in my chest tightening.

"Amma?"

"Mm."

"I lost Appa's car."

"Okay. We'll buy a new one. Appa will be okay."

In her half-sleep she was someplace much better, and

I didn't want her to wake up just yet. I licked my palm again and sucked the nut, playing with it in my mouth. I bit it and chewed slowly, letting the chocolate disappear on my tongue where all that was sweet stayed holy, somewhere inside of me.

92

A day passed by and then another. I stayed inside, hoping the city would forget my face and what had happened. They did.

There were no knocks on my door. There were no phone calls, except from Steph, Toni, and the usual suspects. Mrs. Patrice called and said she'd help buy me a used car—she wasn't keen on building connections with other drivers in the city, ours was a special bond. I said maybe, but I needed more time. Then she promised to mail me that pair of socks she'd knitted.

"I don't want to ruin the surprise, but I can't keep it in much longer."

"What is it, Mrs. P.? You know I've seen all your videos. You're a natural."

"And you're such a charmer, Damani. All right, so on the socks I knitted—"

"No, don't tell me. I love surprises."

She laughed and I realized I'd missed it, so I asked, "How's the sex with the old guy, by the way?" and she laughed some more just for me.

Shereef called me the best loose cannon in history. He

told me about how the people used my car as a barrier. How they set it on fire and barbecued the insides. There was a thirty-second video of people thanking me where I was referred to as "The Taxi Driver."

"There's not a trace of you. Someone removed your VIN tag. The whole thing was incredible. You did something not just anyone can get away with. Everyone at the protest is a suspect."

"I don't believe it. I don't believe any of it," I said, because who the fuck was I but broken? Shereef laughed.

"Trust me. We've got a huge strike plan in motion, by the way. Everyone in transport and gig workers from all over. You'll be there, right?"

In a single night, I became the mysterious poster child for change. At least, that's what Steph had said. The city in the meantime was using what happened to justify bigger bollards. Toni told me that Jolene was raising money for me, but if you ask me, Jolene is the one that needs serious help. Toni had said, "Our emotions are natural responses to an unjust system! Living in our times is a fucking experience! How's her little fundraiser going to change any of that?" She kept reassuring me that no one was disappointed by what I had done. Amma was, though; of course, Stephanie had told her what had happened.

"You can't do those type of things. That smile won't always save you."

Eventually, I felt up to doing a few sets and was lifting heavier than I ever had. Along with the weight training,

I wanted to push myself even more, plus being cooped up inside was a mental strain I couldn't just stretch and make better. As the days dragged by, it was clear that Jolene had no intention of reporting me. She still wanted me to believe that she wasn't like the rest of them.

93

"Damani," called Amma from the kitchen. She was making fish cutlets and the day felt better than the one before. "Look." There was another eviction notice on the table. "The bananas you bought are already black. Make some bread. We don't have any flour, though."

The eviction notice was urgent, all in capitals, boxed, super bold, stark red, and taking up half the page. Money was due three days from now. I never understood why the landlords couldn't just come downstairs and tell us. Clearly they enjoyed using the various font and color functions on their word processor, which was stuck in 1995. How could they have knocked on our door to share some of the cookies they've baked and then slip letters of eviction under our door? Or was I being too extreme again?

I stormed out of our kitchen with the letter in my hand. "Damani! Don't do it." As I stomped my way upstairs to the door, I saw an envelope on the floor half a foot from our shoe mat. "*Damani*" was written on the front in sapphire-blue ink.

The envelope smelled like her. Inside was a wad of cash bundled together with a pink elastic. I could stroke the edges all day with my fingertips. Judging by the thickness and my quick calculations—adding ten times one hundred, plus ten times one hundred about four times, including the smaller bills that stood out in different colors—I knew there was close to eight grand, and it was all ours. I could catch up on rent, even pay some months in advance, sort out my bills, excluding my student loan, of course, treat Steph, Toni, and Shereef to a few feasts, take Amma shopping, and I'd still have a few thousand I could keep towards a food truck. Could I feel good about keeping the money? Absolutely.

Jolene was a sharer, but she'd never fathom giving up all that allowed her to share. There were still millions of little Damanis out there praying money for their parents' bills would fall from the sky or into their mailboxes, postage paid, first class, do not return to sender. Was the eight grand going to make my life a little easier for a while? Yes. But I still would've preferred to have a conversation with Jolene. It felt as if she was trying to sedate me by stuffing copious amounts of money in my mouth. Still, I'd sleep like a fucking baby for once, let's call it compensation.

I ran outside to an empty drive. No one was there.

94

Every Thursday, Shereef stayed over at Stephanie's and slept cozy, cuddling the love of his life. He started giving me the keys to his car those nights, as long as I promised not to drive too fast or into things, especially places deemed important. As a driver himself, he knew we need to drive in order to feel sometimes. Every now and then, I drove to Jolene's place. I parked outside and waited, watching her. In the beginning her curtains were usually closed, but as days passed she started to leave them open again.

On this particular night, she walked up to her window in her sports bra. She looked outside and put her hand in her sweatpants, as if it made her feel safe. It seemed to me that for a brief moment, she saw me. I was looking right at her and I saw her looking back at me, but with all the reflection and darkness, I couldn't be sure. I gripped the car door handle and wanted to open the door, walk straight to her window and touch the glass.

I started the engine and she squinted her eyes, looking closely outside.

Dr. Thelma Hermin Hesse had said in another episode that there was a point we must acknowledge when it is time to move on from unhealthy relationships. "It was when my ex said I could no longer lick the peanut butter off his face that I knew I had to pack my things, leave the ward and move on." Of course, I understood her point, but it was fun imagining that Jolene was in fact looking for me through the spotless glass that separated us. I rolled my windows down and headed to the main road.

95

Not everyone has a Jolene in their life who drops envelopes of "love" at their front door even when they don't ask for it. I had told Amma I'd written a letter to Michael Douglas explaining our situation. He was the one who gave us the cash, and Amma nearly pissed herself. "See, I told you! Michael Douglas is a good guy!" She made me print and frame a picture of him.

We were sitting at Hot Kitchen for the first time since Appa passed away. The aroma of grilled banana peppers, fried potatoes, and vegetables tossed in vinegar and spice filled the restaurant with a familiarity. Amma held the table, eyeing the interior, avoiding looking straight towards the kitchen. She twisted a napkin with both of her hands.

From the back, I smelled frying beef marinated with ginger and garlic. Something was missing and we all knew that. You would never have eaten a sandwich more delicious than Appa's, but I've said that enough, I'm sure.

"Our food's coming."

"Let's go." Amma pushed her seat back ready to leave, but one of the waitresses brought over a pair of sandwiches, a salad, fries, a tea, and a bottle of water. She placed them in front of us and squeezed Amma's shoulder.

"Always in his memory," she said.

"Come on, Ma." We held the warm bread and closed our eyes, each taking a bite. Of course, I was peeking to watch Amma's reaction. Liquid pooled under her lashes, and then a tear fell down her face.

"It's just a sandwich," I reminded her.

"You can be so horrible sometimes," she snapped.

The beef was salty but juicy. The bread was perfectly toasted, and the pepper and secret sauce were refreshing and cool. On my palate was a melding of goodness and memories. I wanted to keep that feeling forever, knowing very well my father was truly gone and that this sandwich was only half as good as his own. I was about to take another bite, but Jolene wouldn't let me savor the moment. That was her coat. That was her hair, her beautiful blonde hair.

She was there, standing in front of Hot Kitchen, after all these months, holding hands with a woman who looked exactly like me from her thrifted clothes to her thick black hair, though she obviously didn't work out. I imagined her name was Shayani. She was a recent veterinarian graduate, certified doctor, her mother's fucking star pillai. The pattern on her tote bag—pop art hamsters with moustaches. Shayani dreamed of opening her own clinic, of course, and Jolene, being so damn lovable, would have taken their meeting as a sign. I saw it so clear right in front of me. The two of them together. Jolene's voice was loud in my head: "*I opened, sorry, we opened this clinic in memory of my dead dog, Hadley.*" She would cry, and Shayani's expertise and hard work would fade into the background. But why would Jolene bring her new girlfriend here, of all the places to dine in the city? "*I once knew a chick whose dad invented this famous sandwich. Hang on, there's some sauce on your face. Babe.*" No, I wasn't jealous, I was going to do what had to be done.

Swallowing the food I had in my mouth, I took a sip of water, then wiped my lips with a napkin.

"Hang on, Ma." I stood up from my chair. "I'll be right back."

Acknowledgments

Your Driver Is Waiting is my debut novel. There are many people to thank without whose energy and commitment this book would not exist.

First, to Bobby Mostyn-Owen. Thank you for pushing and pulling me when and where it mattered most. For your insight and trust, thank you. I'm a better writer having worked with you. You're a star I want to scream about. To both Bobby and James Roxburgh for inviting me to the Atlantic Books Writing Workshop, thank you for that opportunity. James, thank you for the seeds of inspiration and for all the encouragement. I will never get tired of hearing compliments or reading your well-crafted emails. To Mary Chamberlain, thank you for your attention to detail, and for polishing up the page before anyone outside of Atlantic Books had a read. Thank you to Alice Latham for eagerly pushing *Your Driver Is Waiting* to other publishers, and to David Forrer for making the perfect deal. Thank you, Kirsty Doole, for making noise and waves about the book. To Joanna Lee and the entire Atlantic Books team, thank you for all your work and support.

To Margo Shickmanter, for your brilliance and charm.

Our email threads on picking apart the meaning and science of "cuntstruck" and "wet undies": legendary. The behind-the-scenes of writing a novel. It was a dream to work with you in every possible way. To Cara Reilly, thank you for your enthusiasm, comforting kindness, and drive to push the book as far as it can go. Your zen puts me at ease. To Anne Jaconette and Michael Goldsmith, thank you for your thoughtful approach to publicity in the United States, when I felt quite apprehensive. Thank you Rita Madrigal, Chris Jerome, Pei Koay, and Peggy Samedi. So many hands and minds bring a book to life, thank you for all your work towards that. Massive thanks to the entire Doubleday team.

Thank you Nada Hayek and Emily Mahon. I cannot believe a cover can be so badass, and that that cover happens to be mine. You captured the vibe. Thank you.

To Deborah Sun De La Cruz for bringing *Your Driver Is Waiting* to Canada, thank you for your enthusiasm. To Nicole Winstanley, Erin Bonner, Dan French, Bonnie Maitland, and everyone at Penguin Random House in Canada—thank you! To have my novel available in my home city of Tkaronto, Canada, I have no words. Thank you for making this possible. I can't wait to show my nephews it on the shelf.

To my darling Appama, for teaching me to read and write, and for endowing me with your love for writing. I love you.

To my first- and second-grade teacher, Mrs. Carter, and my seventh-grade teacher, Ms. Pearce: Thank you for your encouragement and wisdom. I still use what you taught me about reading and writing to this day. (And I don't just mean finger spacing or indents before starting a new paragraph.) To my twelfth-grade geography/human patterns teacher, Mr. Liapis: Thank you for the time you took to tell me to keep writing, that my writing was "powerful," even when I was close to failing ENG3U and wanted to drop out of school forever.

To Zeyna, thank you for reading my first draft, pouring love into all of your comments, and giving me the surge I needed. To Christine El Kholy, Hesham Zakai, and Nick Dubs (all three writers as well), thank you for reading my outline when I was doubting myself. To Mathumai, thank you for helping me uncover Damani's perfect name. To Gary, thank you for sharing your many stories of driving nights. The pink bird is now memorialized in print. To all the drivers I've ever met and who have shared their stories, and to all workers and nonworkers fighting for their rights and freedom, solidarity. To Rema, though we met after I'd written this novel, thank you for reminding me that while we can all do something towards change, sometimes we have to slow down and hit the brakes.

To Alyia, thank you for your love since 1992. That very auspicious Eid al-Adha night is one I will never forget. Thank you C.N. for being a part of that, and for sharing your love as a car mechanic. Your sobriety is inspiring, brother. Keep at it.

This book would not be what it is without the encouragement of those who have read and supported my previous work. Thank you David Godwin, Merin, Shalini, Alex, V. Geetha, Talah Hassan, and Hesham. To the creative writing faculty at Kingston University and my MA cohort, thank you.

To my elders, aunties, uncles, communities, and all the students I've had thus far, thank you for always teaching me. Tkaronto, a massive shout-out to folks in Scarborough/Rouge River/Malvern/Tuxedo Court. To my dear friend Kris S., thanks for your love and support when I was near rock bottom. You are an incredible human being. To all the friends and souls I've connected with throughout the many cities where I've had the privilege to stay, thank you for always cheering me on no matter how many years it's been. I cherish many memorable moments thanks to you. We had fun.

For this work, I would like to honor A. Sivanandan, Frantz Fanon, and Audre Lorde, as well as Ruby Hamad, whose works helped push my creative process. To all the Black, Indigenous, women of color, and LGBTQI+ folks who have written, fought, performed, and taught before me and with me, thank you for paving the way.

To my family—Amma, Appa, sisters, brothers, and my darling nephews, thank you for giving me the space to create. For our journey, the hours worked, the years dreaming and waiting, thank you for teaching me about love and strength. To Zah and Sal, my angels, what would I do without you? To my comrade and partner G.K., thank you for being my first reader every time, for all our heated conversations on art and life, and for meticulously breaking apart the film *Taxi Driver* with me the first night we watched it together in 2015 and the many times since. For everything and more, thank you. I would not have had the time or room to write as much as I can if it weren't for you.

And to you, dear reader, peace, love, and power. Here's to a new world.